"Jake, I'm so scared. There's more going on here that you need to know."

"What is it?" Jake asked.

"There's something the cartel is after. Something Danny possessed that he hid somewhere in the park. He set up an entire treasure hunt for Austin. And I think at the end he hid whatever the cartel is seeking."

"But how are we supposed to find it?"

"There are clues," Rebecca said. "Clues only Austin can solve. They must have taken him to get me to lead them to whatever Danny hid in the park."

"If that's true, then that's good news," Jake said. "Austin is likely safe as long as he's the leverage they have to get you to comply."

"But the only problem is that Danny designed this scavenger hunt for Austin, not me. There's no way I can solve these clues on my own."

Jake stopped short and turned to put his arm around Rebecca. She buried her head into his shoulder as he squeezed her tight.

"You're not on your own," he whispered. "We're in this together."

Patsy Conway is many things: a writer, a teacher and a soccer coach for his kids. He loves traveling with his family, kayaking on the pond, listening to live music and reading the next great suspense or mystery. Patsy lives in Northeastern Massachusetts with his wife and three boys. This is Patsy's first book. You can connect with the author at patsyconway.com or through the publisher.

Books by Patsy Conway

Love Inspired Suspense

Theme Park Abduction

Visit the Author Profile page at LoveInspired.com.

THEME PARK ABDUCTION

PATSY CONWAY

LOVE INSPIRED SUSPENSE

INSPIRATIONAL ROMANCE

LOVE INSPIRED® SUSPENSE
INSPIRATIONAL ROMANCE

Recycling programs for this product may not exist in your area.

ISBN-13: 978-1-335-58761-9

Theme Park Abduction

For questions and comments about the quality of this book, please contact us at CustomerService@Harlequin.com.

Love Inspired
22 Adelaide St. West, 41st Floor
Toronto, Ontario M5H 4E3, Canada
www.LoveInspired.com

Printed in U.S.A.

Cause me to hear thy lovingkindness in the morning;
for in thee do I trust: cause me to know the way
wherein I should walk; for I lift up my soul unto thee.
—*Psalm* 143:8

This book is dedicated to my wife, Marisa, who made this dream a reality through thousands of edits and countless hours of feedback. I can never thank you enough.

And to my boys, Jack, Will and Oliver, for all of our theme park adventures together. You are my inspiration.

And to my parents and family, for always encouraging and supporting every word I've ever written. I am truly blessed.

ONE

Rebecca Salmon squeezed her nine-year-old son's hand as they rushed up the winding path of the quick-lane entrance for The Screaming Serpent, Adventure World's premiere amusement ride. As Rebecca and Austin scanned their wristbands, she glanced at the line of nearly two hundred people in the stand-by queue, fanning themselves in the sweltering humidity.

Finally, things are going smoothly for us.

The last twenty-four hours had been a nonstop nightmare. Rebecca's brother, Danny, had disappeared abruptly the night before, and she received a phone call from his partner Missy explaining that he had to go back undercover. As an agent for the DEA, Danny kept many secrets from his twin sister, and while this was never easy, she recognized that it was often necessary for their safety. Missy was like an old family friend and was usually so confident and jovial when she spoke to her, but last night as she gave her very specific instructions to follow, she could hear the tremble in her voice.

"Your brother was in possession of something the cartel is after and at the last minute he hid it in the scavenger hunt. Whatever you do, make sure you and Austin see it through to the very end."

As she stood in line at the amusement park, Rebecca looked over her shoulder again to check for anyone suspicious. Her stomach twisted as she considered the impossible task ahead of her. As a child with autism, there was a chance Austin could bolt from her at any time, especially if the lines grew too long and he became impatient. This was why Danny had created the puzzles for him to solve as they made their way through the park. Austin was so excited for this scavenger hunt, but would they be able to tackle all these clues and find what Danny had hidden at the end of his game?

"Please, God," she prayed. "Give me the strength to stay calm and focused. For Austin."

As she opened her eyes, Rebecca felt relief when the line began to move and Austin bounced beside her with pure joy and excitement. If he was sensing Rebecca's fear, it was not impacting his behavior. At least not yet.

Adventure World truly was the world's greatest theme park, and the accessibility options for children like Austin were incredible. Since his diagnosis at age two, it had been a struggle to bring him to a crowded place. On their first trip here, six years ago, Austin had bolted from his stroller, and Rebecca and her late husband, Corey, spent most of the afternoon chasing after their three-year-old. He was less likely to run off now, but she still grasped him tightly him by the hand just in case.

In her other hand she held the first clue that Danny had left for them to solve. Back home they played these escape room–style games, and he'd designed the ultimate challenge for his nephew set against the magnificent backdrop of Adventure World.

But now, instead of the typical toy or prize for Austin to find when he cracked that last lock, Danny had hidden something the cartel was after—and finding it first was the only way for Rebecca to keep them safe.

She stared at the clue in her hand and tried to make sense of the message.

Ride the Serpent that is not venomous, the color is true, and there, underneath, you'll find the next clue.

It was still as enigmatic as when she'd first read it, but Austin had figured it out almost instantly. He had an amazing knowledge of facts and figures that far exceeded the understanding of most nine-year-olds. He was fascinated with Adventure World and knew the dates when every ride opened and closed and when they underwent renovations. As soon as Rebecca read him the clue, he'd started off in the direction of this roller coaster without a word. It made sense to Rebecca that the answer lay somewhere within the Screaming Serpent ride, but she could not figure out what was meant by "the color is true"? But Austin knew.

As they reached the front of the line, the operator gestured to the red copperhead coaster with her outstretched arm. But Austin remained frozen in place and tugged on his mother's hand as she attempted to move forward.

"We have to wait," he said. "Copperheads are poisonous."

Rebecca knew this was not worth arguing about, so

she signaled to the families behind them to go on ahead. When the yellow rattlesnake car approached, Rebecca hoped that he would be ready to proceed, but as she pulled at his wrist, Austin's feet remained glued to the floor. When the green python approached, she could feel her own anxiety rising as she imagined the worst-case scenario in which Austin refused to comply and she would have to pick him up and carry him, kicking and screaming, back down the ramp. But just as Rebecca was about to give up and start escorting him to the exit, the blue python coaster pulled up and the tension in Austin's grasp eased as he happily took his mother's hand and guided them toward the middle seats of the car. As soon as they climbed into the car, Austin knelt on the floor and reached as far as he could under the seat.

"What are you doing, Austin? Sit up. They won't let us go if you don't sit up and fasten your belt."

As Austin straightened up, he held out his hand to show her a small, folded triangle of paper that reminded Rebecca of the notes she passed in school as a child.

"Is that Uncle Danny's clue?"

"Yes, he said it would be under the seat. Pythons are not poisonous. And the color was true. True blue, like Uncle Danny."

Rebecca smiled and kissed her son on the forehead. The clue finally made sense to her, and she marveled at how easily the answer had come to Austin. Since her husband had died in the crash two years ago, Danny had stepped up to become an even bigger presence in her boy's life. He would write clues on paper, send text messages or utilize all the latest gadgets and technology to create these riddles for his nephew. The clues would lead to combinations for locked boxes that held a prize, usually something simple like a Matchbox car or toy train. Rebecca knew Austin would love that Danny had created a hunt set against the backdrop of Adventure World, which was Austin's favorite place on earth.

But this was no longer a child's game, and their lives depended upon solving these riddles. Suddenly the stakes were real.

Her brother had been undercover with the Velázquez cartel along with his partners Lance and Missy. In the past few days Danny had started to question everything and everyone and believed that someone on his team had flipped and was working for the cartel. Danny was careful not share any more with Rebecca than she needed to know, but whatever the cartel was after was now hidden at the end of the scavenger hunt.

Austin unfolded the next clue, and Rebecca sipped her water as she attempted to read it over his shoulder.

"What does it say?" Rebecca asked.

Austin read from the scrap of paper in his hand. "'If Delaware is number one and Massachusetts is number six, then where you are now will admittedly lead you to the first combination.'"

Rebecca took the paper from her son and reread the clue. She shook her head at the awkward phrasing. "I have no idea what this means—do you?"

"It's Florida," he said. "That's where we are now."

"Okay, but what about those numbers? Why is Delaware number one?"

Austin giggled as the Adventure World ride operator checked their shoulder harnesses and locked them in place.

"Delaware was the first state to be *admitted* to the United States. And Massachusetts was the sixth," he said. "So the combination is related to Florida and the date it joined the union. Florida was admitted on March 3, 1845."

The ride operator smiled, nodding her head in awe at Austin's remarkable recitation of facts.

"He knows his stuff," Rebecca said as the operator gave a tug on the bar that pressed against Rebecca's chest.

"So where will we find this first combination?" Rebecca whispered to Austin.

"The Hall of Flags, silly," he said as the Screaming Serpent jerked into motion.

Rebecca kissed her son gently on the top of his curly head as the roller coaster car began its climb toward the top of the incline.

"You're amazing, you know that?"

"I know," Austin said. "You're amazing, too. Once we're off this ride, we can head straight there for the next clue."

The coaster creaked as it inched its way up the summit. Rebecca could see the big drop ahead, and she clenched Austin's wrist with one hand and made a fist with the other, digging her nails into her palm. With every shake and vibration, her anxiety intensified as her stomach began to drop. She exhaled slowly as she heard a loud screech, and then the car whipped to the right and then back to the left before dropping into a free fall.

Everyone screamed.

Terror ripped through Rebecca's body and froze her for a moment. She was not a fan of roller coasters or even bumper cars. The Ferris wheel was more her speed. But Austin loved them, and she would do anything to provide him with a sense of normalcy through all this.

But as the coaster dipped down into its final turn, Rebecca heard more cries than expected coming from the people in the cars behind her. Something was wrong.

They were moving too fast. The traction felt loose. She felt a sudden jerk and then heard a loud, piercing squeal. Then, just as they entered into the tunnel, their cars slammed to a halt.

Rebecca reached with both hands for Austin's arms and squeezed him tight. She leaned into his blond curls and kissed him again on top of his head.

"It's okay," she whispered. "It's going to be all right."

But Rebecca's confidence was short-lived. She heard another loud shriek from the back of the car, as if the brakes were coming loose. The coaster cars rattled and all the lights went out, leaving them in complete darkness. Soon the emergency lights blinked on, and the loudspeakers apologized for the "technical difficulties causing this accidental delay." But Rebecca feared that this was no accident.

Could this be the cartel?

Last night, when her brother's partner Missy told her that Danny was going back undercover, she had clearly been worried and confused. Missy had made her promise not to trust anyone until they reunited.

"Danny was clear in his instructions," Missy said. "Just go to the park, have a great day and solve every clue. And he will be back before you know it."

Rebecca's first instinct was to lock down in the hotel room until he returned safely. But Danny was adamant that she would be safest in the park. This was correct for so many reasons, the most obvious being the reality that if she had to convince Austin of a change in plans of this magnitude without any warning, it would be nearly impossible. Austin knew every second of their itinerary for the day, and he had to be on line for the roller coaster at exactly 8:00 a.m. So Missy had suggested she would call in a favor and have someone keep an eye on them.

"I don't need protecting," Rebecca insisted. "And I don't need some DEA contact from Florida who doesn't know me following me around all day."

"Take the help," Missy had said. "Don't be so stubborn."

"I'll be fine," she said. "I'm pretty tough. Plus, didn't you just tell me not to trust anyone?"

After that exchange Missy had backed off. She had hit a nerve. Missy herself offered to come down all the way from Boston, but Rebecca assured her she would be fine. After she hung up with Missy, she watched the local news and drifted off to sleep.

It only took one look at Austin's enthusiastic face for her to find the strength to pull it together and journey into Adventure World. And everything had been going so well. Until now.

The darkness in the roller coaster tunnel was pierced by the light from the passengers illuminating their mobile phones. On her own device, Rebecca slid her thumb up from the bottom of the screen and pressed on the symbol for the flashlight. In the soft glow, she saw her son rocking in his own arms, his head buried in his chest.

"What's going on?" he asked. "Why did they stop the ride?"

"It's fine, honey," Rebecca said. "They'll get us off here soon."

But the rocking only intensified. Rebecca knew these behaviors well. Change was difficult for him, and so much was happening too fast. Without warning, the bar that had been pushing up against Rebecca's chest and holding them in place unlocked and slowly drifted forward. She dropped her phone while she grasped the bar with one hand and reached for Austin with the other.

"That's not supposed to happen," said Austin. "Mom? Why did that just happen?"

The emergency lights flickered on and off as a robotic voice called from the loudspeaker, "Attention. Please exit the vehicle immediately and proceed to the emergency exits along the right side of the tunnel."

Rebecca felt Austin's body tensing in her arms. He had watched hundreds of videos of the Screaming Serpent to prepare for this ride, creating a social story so that he could adjust to this new environment. He knew every twist and turn and anticipated the animatronic characters' lines before they spoke. Any unexpected change in their plans could be incredibly difficult for him, and she knew that his anxiety fed off her own. She knew that if he panicked, he could throw a tantrum or even freeze and refuse to move to a place of safety. Rebecca braced for the worst. He was too big now for her to pick him up, and this noise and excitement could make him start to scream. Rebecca closed her eyes and spoke the words she had prayed so many times. "Oh Lord, help guide and protect us."

At that moment, Rebecca felt a vibration on her lap. The muffled buzzing of her phone immediately caught her son's attention, bringing him back into the moment.

"Is that a message?" he asked. "From Uncle Danny? Could it be another one of his clues?"

"It could be," Rebecca said. "He's always one step ahead."

"Can I see it?" Austin asked, motioning for her phone.

"Not right now, honey. But as soon as we go on a little detour, we can read the message."

"Is this a part of the game?" Austin asked. "Going on a little detour?"

She realized that following this line of thinking was the best possible way to bring his anxiety, as well as her own, back down to earth. So Rebecca played along.

"Yes, honey, we are going to climb out now and go on a little detour."

"Just a little detour," Austin echoed.

His repetition was a good sign, as this usually signified that he was accepting the unexpected change in plans. *Thank God. We're going to be okay.*

As the other passengers exited the coaster and proceeded cautiously behind the animatronic figures who were eerily frozen in midperformance, Rebecca instructed Austin to climb out of the car while she scanned her flashlight under their seats to make sure they had left nothing behind. She was immediately glad that she did this, because she found his fidget toy on the floor of the coaster car, an item that Austin would have been devastated to leave behind.

But her joy was fleeting. When she looked up, she noticed that Austin had already moved quite far ahead of her, following the white arrows that illuminated the ground and ducking under the arms of those ahead of him.

"Austin! Wait!" Rebecca yelled as she shoved her phone into the back pocket of her shorts and leaped out of the car. "Wait!"

But her nine-year-old was still small enough to sneak under the clasped hands of the passengers, and he scooted between everyone too quickly to be stopped. As she pushed through the crowd, she tried to keep her eyes on him as he began to disappear. And then, just as Rebecca finally caught a glimpse of him again, she saw a tall man in a red polo shirt put his hand on Austin's shoulder and guide him forward toward the exit. Rebecca shrieked her son's name as the emergency lights blinked off. The entire space was now engulfed in darkness as Austin disappeared through the doors with the stranger.

Rebecca extended her hands as if she were blind-folded and called Austin's name as she pushed her way through the darkness. But she never heard her son re-spond.

At that moment she felt another vibration in her pocket and was reminded of the message waiting for her. *Not now*, she thought. *Not now, Danny!*

She was angry with him for leaving them alone today, but all that she could think about was getting to Austin. *Please, God, help me find my son.*

As she made it through the doors and into the bright sun, her phone buzzed again, but this time Rebecca had a different thought. What if this was the GPS locator Austin was carrying? Before they left for Adventure World, she had purchased this system that was specif-ically designed for children with special needs. With the push of a button, Austin could immediately check in to let his mother know his location. The gadget also had geo-fencing capabilities, so if Austin ever left a defined location, Rebecca's phone would buzz. There were other features as well, like the ability to ring an alarm to help find him in a crowd, and another option that let her drop in and listen to Austin's surroundings. Rebecca knew she had clipped the GPS tracker to his shoe that morning and tested it before they left for breakfast, and they'd even reviewed how he could use it if he ever got lost.

As she reached into her pocket to retrieve her phone, she prayed that there would be a signal from her son telling her where he was so that she could find him safe and sound.

She clicked on the message and read the most terrifying words just as the screen flickered and turned to black. A large red battery signal appeared, and Rebecca hit the home button repeatedly, but nothing happened. Using the flashlight in the darkness must have drained her battery and the backup charger she'd packed was in Austin's backpack. Her phone was dead, her son was gone, and she had just read the four most horrific words a mother could ever imagine.

WE HAVE YOUR SON.

Jake Foster stood tall and arched his shoulders back as he craned his neck to see what was happening ahead. When the lights went out, he had lost sight of Rebecca in the darkness, but he pushed through the crowds to make his way outside, and now he could see a glimpse of her up ahead, calling out for her son.

"Rebecca! Is everything okay? It's me, Jake. Jake Foster."

Jake removed his sunglasses and sensed that Rebecca recognized his face as she processed hearing this name from her past.

"Jake?" she said. "What are you doing here?"

Jake wanted to tell her that Danny had called him last

night, told him he was going back undercover with the cartel and asked him to follow her and keep her safe. Since Jake worked for the FBI out of the Orlando office in the division of violence against children, he was the perfect person to watch over her, but he knew that Rebecca had wanted nothing to do with having anyone there to protect her. So Danny made Jake promise to make any interactions with her appear to be a coincidence. It pained him to be anything less than completely honest with Rebecca, but Danny had warned him that she would not trust him if she knew he was there on Danny's orders.

"My friend asked me to come here today," Jake said in an attempt to not stray too far from the truth. "And when I heard someone screaming, I realized it was you."

"It's my son," Rebecca said. "This man in a red polo shirt with dark hair and a mustache took him when the lights went out. And now they've got him."

"Who's got him?" Jake asked.

"The cartel," Rebecca whispered. "Danny has been undercover with the DEA, and he has something the cartel wants. First he disappeared last night and went back undercover and now they are after us."

"Are you certain?"

"The kidnappers texted me, just before my phone died." Rebecca said. "It must be the cartel. They have Austin."

"Let's get to park security now. In these situations, every second counts."

Jake pointed to a sign that was marked Exit and led her down a ramp and through a winding path. He leaped over the stanchions and directed her to do the same. So much about this situation bothered him. His conversation with Danny had been so brief, and now he wished he had taken the time to gather more information when they spoke last night that could help explain more about this sudden turn of events. But there was no time now for him to contemplate these questions.

"This way," Jake said as they sped through the main exit and through the gift shop. Up ahead a woman in a royal blue Adventure World shirt waved to flag them down. She spoke into her walkie-talkie, and as they approached Jake noticed that her name badge read Charlene.

"Is everything okay here?" Charlene asked.

"No," Rebecca said. "My son is missing. He's been kidnapped."

"Kidnapped? Okay, miss. No worries. He's probably just run on ahead. Happens all the time."

"No. I got a message on my phone that he's been taken."

Rebecca looked down at the unresponsive device in her hand.

"Do you have a charger or anything I can use to power up? I have a GPS system on my phone, and I can use that to track him," Rebecca asked.

"I'm sorry. The security team doesn't have anything like that. One of the gift shops might have something?"

"I have no time to search for a charger—my son is in danger!"

Jake furrowed his brow as he listened. It seemed odd that this security guard couldn't be more helpful. To her credit, Charlene kept cool and tried her best to calm Rebecca's nerves. "Don't worry, miss. We will find him. What is his name?"

"Austin. He's nine years old, and he's autistic."

"And what is he wearing?"

"I dressed him in fluorescent green from head to toe. Even his sneakers are iridescent."

Charlene cupped her hand above her eyes as if she was looking into the distance. "Does your son have curly hair?" she asked. "Blond?"

"Yes." Rebecca's voice intensified. "Have you seen him?"

"I saw a boy fitting that description come off the ride with a man in red that I thought was his father. He was moving his hands rapidly and flapping his arms."

"That's him," Rebecca said. "Where did he go?"

Charlene pointed behind them to the left. "They exited the gift shop and took off toward the Old West Ghost Town."

"What?" Rebecca said. "Okay. Thank you so much."

"If you see him first, just stay put, find any park crew member and radio it in," Charlene said. "If I find him, I'll bring him to Guest Services. Will you and your husband be splitting up or looking together?"

Rebecca turned to look at Jake. "Oh, he's not my husband. He's just—"

"A friend." Jake interrupted her midsentence. "And I'll be helping her until Austin is safe and sound."

They made full eye contact for the first time, and as she brushed a panicked tear from her eye, Rebecca smiled and mouthed the words *thank you*.

Charlene lifted the walkie-talkie to her lips to begin to call this in, and Jake signaled to Rebecca that they should head in the direction of the ghost town. Within a few steps, their pace increased from a light jog to a slow run.

Thoughts raced through Jake's mind. Danny had

made him promise to watch over and protect Rebecca and Austin no matter what and to make sure they followed all the clues for this elaborate scavenger hunt that he had devised. He stressed that they would be safest in the park, and that it was so important that they followed every clue. It all sounded like a game, just another diversion at Adventure World. Of course, now Jake wished he had asked Danny where he had buried whatever it was the cartel was after. But when they spoke Danny hadn't mentioned anything about a potential kidnapping. His old friend could not have known that Rebecca and Austin would find themselves in this kind of danger, could he?

As he glanced over at the woman running beside him, Jake admired the determination that Rebecca had when it came to finding her son. She had kicked it into another gear. It was more than the speed at which she was moving; it encompassed her entirely.

And being mistaken for Rebecca's husband had made Jake feel more alive than he had since his fiancée, Alyssa, left him last summer. But this was no time to be thinking of Rebecca in this way. They had to find her son, and he could not let himself lose sight of that.

As they approached the wooden sign for the Old West Ghost Town, Rebecca stopped to catch her breath. She pointed to the riverboat that was loading passengers to her left.

"What if they took Austin to the island?" she asked. "Or he could be in the ghost town! If we choose wrong, I may never see him again."

"Maybe we should split up?" Jake suggested. "We could cover more ground that way."

"But if you find Austin, how will you let me know? My phone is dead."

"Here," Jake said, handing her his phone and motioning to his wrist. "I've got a smart watch. I can make calls from here, and we can use the two-way feature to communicate with each other."

"Perfect," she said. "I'll go left toward the cemetery, and you jump on that boat for the island. Either way, let's meet back here in fifteen minutes," she said, pointing to the facade of the post office they were passing.

"Gotcha," said Jake, raising his hand to his midchest. "Green shirt, curly hair, about this high?"

Rebecca nodded, veering her steps to the left. "That's Austin."

Jake turned and ran to the riverboat and sneaked on just as they closed the stanchion. He made his way to the stern, and as the boat pulled away from the dock, he kept his eyes on Rebecca and watched as she raced over the hill before she disappeared from his sight.

Only then did he notice she was being followed.

TWO

Rebecca felt a burning in her calves as her feet pounded the pavement, but the adrenaline pumping through her kept her moving. If Austin was still in the park, then she had to find him before the kidnappers made their escape. Her mind raced as she wondered why they would take him. Typically kidnappers demanded a ransom, but there was nothing she or Austin had that would be of any value. She realized that they must believe she had whatever was at the end of the scavenger hunt in her possession already, but what they didn't know was that she would never be able to solve the clues without Austin by her side.

As her mind raced through the possibilities, she also began to think about Jake Foster. There were over fifty thousand guests crowding into Adventure World every day. What were the chances that she would bump into him? It was a major coincidence, and she didn't believe in coincidences. But then she remembered her prayers. Maybe Jake was God's way of intervening.

Rebecca would be the first to admit that years ago she had a crush on her brother's best friend, but those feelings had never amounted to more than some fun summer evenings at the movies when they were teen-agers. And to be honest, she always felt like Jake had abandoned them when he returned home from his tour in Afghanistan, moving to Florida and basically disap-pearing from their lives.

She had not seen him much in those years and only heard the highlights of his life through her brother. Medal of valor in the war. Promotions at the FBI. She knew he had a serious girlfriend at one time. Was he married now? Did Jake know that she was a widow?

But Rebecca immediately dismissed these thoughts from her mind. Corey had been a great husband and fa-ther, but she had promised herself after his death that her number one focus had to always be on her son—no dating, no distractions. Austin needed her. And he'd never needed her more than he did right now.

Up ahead she saw the pillory and stocks with fami-lies posing for pictures, and she turned right and headed for the center of the ghost town. Out of the corner of her eye, she saw a flash of green dash out of the rear en-trance of the sarsaparilla café and dart under the bridge, heading north toward the old haunted cemetery. Could that be Austin?

Even though she had been running for ten minutes, somehow Rebecca found more speed as she bolted past the young families holding hands and dodging between the motor scooters driven by elderly couples in match-ing Adventure World T-shirts and hats. Rebecca was in good shape and navigated the terrain well, keeping her gaze fixed on that flash of green.

The dusty asphalt of the Old West Ghost Town under her feet soon gave way to the grass of the haunted cem-etery as the boy made his way up through the tombstones toward the line that was queuing up for the ride. As she got closer, Rebecca noticed that the boy seemed to have curly hair, but she lost sight of him momentarily as he ran behind the large hedges that comprised a mazelike structure around the grounds of the Princess's Castle. The phone she clenched in her fist began to vibrate. It was Jake.

Rebecca answered quickly.

"Change of plans," she said. "I may have spotted Austin."

"Where are you?" Jake asked.

"Heading toward the Haunted Castle."

"Rebecca," Jake said. "Be careful. There's a man in a red polo following behind you."

Rebecca turned her head and recognized the same man from the roller coaster—the man who took Austin. He was gaining on her and moved his hand behind him as if reaching for a weapon. Did he have a gun?

Rebecca leaped over the hedges to her right and made her way into the maze of bushes surrounding the cemetery. The crowds were lighter this morning, and the park was not using the entire queue as it did at its busiest times. Rebecca turned left, then right, making her way around one end of the maze. The hedges were now at least eight feet high, and Rebecca could not see anything other than a glimpse of the castle up ahead on the hill.

The man followed her into the maze and shouted at her to stop. They were inside the maze now, out of sight of most of the crowd, and when she glanced back at him, he raised his gun in her direction. How could he have smuggled a weapon like that inside Adventure World? But she did not have time to think.

Rebecca dived directly into the bushes and pushed

her way through to the other side. She reversed directions and then leaped back into the queue, pushing her way under the wooden railing and immersing herself in the crowds. She never looked back, and in a few moments Rebecca had created a safe distance for herself. For now she had avoided the worst, but she'd completely lost sight of the boy in green she was following and realized that nothing could be worse than never seeing her son again.

Jake pushed his way to the bow to find the captain and make him turn the boat around.

"Sir, we need to go back to the other shore. I have to get off. It's an emergency."

"This riverboat is just like any other ride at the park. It moves back and forth across the lake on a track."

"The tracks run that deep?"

"Not as deep as you think," the captain said. "It's all an optical illusion. Water's only about four feet deep. We keep it dark and murky like that so it looks like it's over fifty."

That was all the information Jake needed to hear.

He raced back to the stern and flipped himself over the edge and jumped into the water. Guests from all decks began to scream and point.

"I'm okay," Jake called out. "I'm with the FBI and this is an emergency."

He jogged through the water, which only came up to his chest—and surely spoiled the illusion for the guests. As he approached the shore, he scaled the ravine and felt the squish of the muck from the lake in his shoes. His shorts and T-shirt would dry quickly in this hot sun, but his sneakers would be another matter entirely. As he reached the top, he climbed over the rope to find two Adventure World security employees there to arrest him.

"Stop right there, sir," shouted a female security guard. She put her hand on his shoulder while her partner patted him down.

"You don't understand," Jake said. "Someone's life is in danger." As they searched his body for weapons, Jake thought about his gun that he had checked in at the front gate. Only on-duty law enforcement with jurisdiction in the park could carry a weapon inside, but he knew the cartel could have found a way around those rules. The bad guys always did. Now he wished he had it with him for protection.

"What do you mean, sir? Who is in danger?"

"My son," Rebecca said as she appeared from behind him. "He's nine years old, and he's been kidnapped."

"Ma'am, my name is Rhonda. We help parents find their missing children every day. But that doesn't explain why this man illegally jumped out of the boat into Adventure Lake."

"He's not missing," Jake pleaded. "He's been kidnapped. And I'm with the FBI." He reached into his back pocket and pulled out his credentials and showed both Rhonda and her partner, who took them in his hands for closer inspection.

"We haven't received any alerts on this," Rhonda said as she began typing on her tablet. "What is your child's name?"

"Austin," Rebecca said. "Austin Salmon. Like the fish. Didn't Charlene call this in?"

Rhonda looked up from her tablet.

"I'm sorry, but nothing has been called in for any

missing children today. We receive an immediate Code Adam whenever there is a report."

"What?" Jake shouted, raising his voice. "That's impossible. We reported him to that woman as soon it happened. Do you mean you haven't been looking for him all this time?"

"Sir, I'm going to have to ask you to keep your voice down."

"I'm not sure you understand," Rebecca interjected. "He is autistic, and he ran off and I saw a man put his hands on him and…"

Rebecca burst into tears, and Jake reached out and pulled her close. Rhonda typed and scrolled on the screen and then turned it around to show them a picture of a boy with bright blue eyes and curly golden hair.

"That's him," Rebecca said. "How do you have his picture?"

"You registered him with guest services," Rhonda said. "When you mentioned he was autistic, I figured it was worth a chance to search the database. Says here that he's a runner. Any chance he just took off?"

"No," Jake said. "The kidnappers texted Rebecca and told her they had her son."

Rhonda leaned into her shoulder and made the call on her two-way radio. "Attention, all security, we have a Code Adam." As she provided all the details, the other guard spoke to Jake and Rebecca and returned Jake's FBI credentials to him.

"Mr. Foster, we now have every employee in the park on high alert. Security guards are at every exit, and we will not let anyone leave until the boy is found. Now could you tell me, are you the boy's father?"

"No," Jake said. "Just a friend."

"So what about his father? Is he here? Could he be involved?"

"He died about two years ago," Rebecca said.

"I'm sorry, ma'am. It's just that in these cases it's so often about the family."

Jake considered how much he should tell these security guards and wondered if Rebecca knew how much to hold back. If they provided too little detail, they would not understand the urgency and would be standing around here all day. But if they told them too much, it could put Rebecca and Austin in even greater danger. He decided to take the lead for now. No mention of the cartel.

"Yes, I work in the crimes against children division. It's the family eighty percent of the time. But not this time. She received a threatening text, and we need to find out who sent it."

"May I see the message?" the guard asked.

Rebecca held her phone out from her pocket.

"I need to get this thing powered up."

Rhonda reached into a pouch on her hip and fished through it to produce a battery-powered phone charger. She handed it to Rebecca, who immediately plugged in her own device and waited for the power to slowly return.

"This happens all the time," Rhonda said. "All park security now carry universal backup chargers."

Jake wondered why Charlene had never offered them one, but as he looked at the red battery light on her dark phone, he realized that the kidnappers might already be trying to contact her again. She needed to get back to a full charge soon.

"Thank you," Rebecca said. "This is a lifesaver."

"Now your son," Rhonda continued, "it says here you have a GPS tracker for him?"

Jake noticed how Rebecca's eyes lit up with the return of the slightest bit of hope.

"Of course," she said. "I'd completely forgotten all about it. My brother's partner from work Missy recommended we get one for him before we came to Adventure World. It's a small tracker that's in his shoe."

"Great," Jake said. "Is there a way we can access it?"

Rebecca looked back down to the still-lifeless but charging phone in her hand.

"Not until this gets to at least fifteen percent," she said. "There's an app on here that will tell us exactly where he is. It even plays a sound when he is close. But you have to be within one hundred yards for that to work."

"Thank you, Mrs. Salmon," Rhonda said. "Now, can you tell me more about what he is wearing today?"

As Rebecca spoke, Rhonda immediately repeated every detail into her walkie-talkie for the Adventure World security team. Jake was impressed with the details Rebecca had considered—every article of clothing was chosen with safety in mind. Suddenly, he heard a buzzing coming from the phone in Rebecca's hand. It had just enough juice to power on, and it immediately showed that she had a missed text message.

Rebecca flicked her thumb from the bottom of the screen and quickly entered her pass code. Jake's heart raced as he watched her press the button to enlarge the message. From the look on her face, he could immediately tell that the news was not good. He took the phone from her as she buried her face in her hands and cried.

Jake read the kidnapper's message, scrolling in capital letters across the screen, and immediately felt his heart drop in his chest.

TALK TO PARK SECURITY AND YOU'LL NEVER SEE HIM ALIVE AGAIN.

THREE

Rebecca grabbed the phone from Jake's hand and started to back away from the guards.

"I'm sorry," she said. "We need to be going."

"You're not going anywhere," Rhonda said. "We need to get you two to the front gates, to our headquarters right away."

Rebecca shared the screen for the security guards to read.

"We've already said too much. If they're watching us, they already know." Her eyes began to well up as she imagined the very worst happening to her son.

She looked to Jake for direction. She could not believe how fortunate she was that God had led him to her in this hour of desperation, and she needed him to be her rock.

"Thank you," Jake said to Rhonda, "but we need to do this on our own now."

"Well, I'm at least going to help you. You can take the shortcut to the front through the employees-only passage." She gestured toward a side gate marked Adventure World Staff Only.

Jake took Rebecca's hand and squeezed, his blue eyes focused intently on her own.

"What's done is done," he said. "If they're on the same channel, they know that we've put out a call for his safety. I think the best thing now is to get to the main security house so I can retrieve my gun and then we can figure this out from there."

Rhonda walked them over to the entrance to the employee passage and scanned her badge to open the gate.

"I wish you all the best," she said. "I'll keep you in my thoughts."

As soon as they stepped through the gate and Rhonda shut the door behind them, Rebecca was startled to realize the stark contrast in their surroundings. Immediately they were transported from the Old West and back to reality. Now that they were behind the scenes, the stunning illusions and forced perspective of the theme park were replaced by the cold, industrial feel of this backstage world. The majestic mountains and castles did not look so magnificent from behind. The false walls and artificial structures resembled the phony props on the stage of a high school play. But the most striking difference for Rebecca was that they had gone so quickly from being on a street crowded with thousands of guests to a nearly empty path where they were essentially all alone.

But with Jake by her side, Rebecca felt protected. It was strange to her how easily she found herself trusting him, since she never allowed herself to open up like that to anyone. Her father had left when she and Danny were babies, and her mother raised them on her own, despite being nearly blind from diabetes by the time Rebecca was in high school. And Rebecca had dropped out of college after a year to take care of her mother before she died. Within months of her passing, Rebecca sold the family house, found a small apartment for Danny and herself, and took on a full-time job to pay the rent. By the end of the year, Corey had proposed, and she was pregnant with Austin the next spring.

It hurt when Jake returned home from overseas but never resumed his place in their lives. Jake had been such an important part of her high school years—they'd been so close—and today she felt herself opening up to him even though she knew it was ridiculous, surely just her emotional response to the worst scenario she could ever imagine.

It was true, none of the tragedies she faced before consumed her as much as losing her child. When her husband had died in the car accident, Rebecca had been devastated. It did not seem fair that her father could abandon her and she could lose her mother at such a young age and then become a widow left alone to raise her child. Rebecca could have lost her faith in God, but instead, somehow, these trials made her even stronger. And now, at her very darkest moment, God had brought Jake back to her after all these years. *What a blessing*, she thought. *Just when I need him the most.*

"Jake, I'm so scared. There's more going on here that we need to figure out."

"What is it?" Jake asked.

"There's something the cartel is after. Something Danny possessed that he hid somewhere in the park."

"What is it and why would he hide it here?"

"I don't know what it is, but I can only imagine that Danny had no choice and hid it before he ran out of time. This is going to sound strange, but he set up an entire treasure hunt for Austin here in the park. And I think he buried whatever the cartel is seeking at the end."

"But Adventure World is over twenty-five thousand acres. How are we supposed to find it?"

"There are clues," Rebecca said, her voice stuttering as her thoughts returned to her boy. "Clues only Austin can solve."

"But why wouldn't Danny have just brought whatever it is to the proper authorities? Why would he keep it here and put you in harm's way?"

"I've been asking myself the same thing. It's the opposite of how he operates. He usually keeps us completely in the dark, since the less we know, the less danger we will ever find ourselves in."

"Maybe there's more going on here than we realize?"

"But why would they kidnap Austin?" Rebecca asked before answering her own question. "They must have taken him to get me to lead them to whatever Danny hid in the park."

"If that's true, then that's good news," Jake said, "Austin is likely safe as long as he's the leverage they have to get you to comply."

"But the only problem is that Danny designed this scavenger hunt for Austin, not me. There's no way I can solve these clues on my own."

Jake stopped short and turned to put his arm around Rebecca and pulled her toward him for a hug. She was startled by the gesture, but it felt so incredible to be in his arms. She buried her head into his shoulder as he squeezed her tight.

"You're not on your own," he whispered. "We're in this together."

Rebecca closed her eyes, just for a moment, and found strength in his words. But as soon as she opened them, she saw a quick wave of motion flash from behind them as a dark figure charged in their direction.

"Look out!" she yelled.

Jake instinctively pivoted to the right and moved her safely out of the way just as the man began reaching into the breast pocket of his Adventure World security uniform. Jake stepped into his path and bumped him squarely in the chest. As the man fell to his knees, he pulled a knife from a hidden sheath and swiped at Jake's ankle. Jake leaped forward, avoiding the blade, and landed a forceful kick into the assailant's arm, causing him to drop his weapon.

Rebecca screamed and ran to the knife and booted it out of reach and into the bushes.

"Call for help," Jake yelled to Rebecca as he grabbed the attacker by the wrist and wrapped the man's arm around his back, pushing his knee into his thigh and forcing him facedown on the ground. In one motion Jake climbed on top of the man and twisted his other arm behind his back.

"Rhonda," Rebecca yelled as she ran back toward the gate. "Somebody help us!"

There was no one to hear her, but Rebecca noticed a security call box posted by the side of the path and pushed the buttons furiously. She reported their location to security before sprinting back to Jake, who has firmly on the back of their assailant and well underway in his questioning.

"Who are you? What are you after?" Jake asked.

The man spoke in muffled Spanish, a language that Rebecca knew well enough to understand, but she could not make out anything he was mumbling.

"Memoria USB," the man said.

"What's that?" Rebecca asked.

"He said, 'Memoria USB,'" Jake said. "Like a USB stick?"

"Give it to me," the man said. "Or else."

"Or else what?" Jake asked, tightening his grip on the man's arms, causing him to wince in pain. But before he could answer, the Adventure World security guards Rebecca had summoned were now standing behind him and put their hands on Jake's shoulders.

"He attacked us," Rebecca said to the guards. "With a knife. Why would one of your guards attack us?"

"He's not one of us," the guard said as he took a pair of restraints from his belt. After handcuffing the man on the ground, they helped Jake to his feet.

Rebecca rushed into Jake's arms and buried her head in his chest.

"Thank God," she said, "for saving us."

"We're nowhere near safe yet," Jake said. "How did he get that weapon in here?"

"That's nothing," she said. "The one who chased me through the maze had a gun."

"A gun? You're sure?"

"I'm sure. These are seriously bad people. All I know is that we have to find this flash drive now on our own," she whispered. "We can't waste time going to security. Whatever is on that drive is the only thing they want, and finding it is the one way I get Austin back safe and sound."

"Okay," Jake said. "So how do we do that?"

Rebecca dug her hand into her pocket.

"This is the clue Austin and I were following. I think you and I have to figure this out on our own."

Jake looked at Rebecca and then turned his attention to the security team.

"You all go on ahead. We're a little shaken up, and so we are going to catch our breath and then meet you at main security."

"Sir," the guard said. "Protocol states we can't leave you alone."

"Look," Jake said as he pulled his FBI credentials from his pocket. "Believe me, I'm a rule follower. But I'm ready to throw that book out the window. You have to trust us to do the right thing here."

Rebecca sensed that the guard was reluctant to agree, but Jake was not giving in.

"Okay, but promise me you'll make your way to main security as soon as you can. Since you're with the FBI, that's the only reason I'm not insisting we stay with you at all times."

Jake and Rebecca thanked them. But as soon as the guards were out of sight, Rebecca showed Jake the folded paper clue.

"The last thing Austin told me was that we needed to go to the Hall of Flags. To find something about Florida and when it became a state."

But as she spoke, the phone in her pocket began to buzz, and Rebecca's heart froze.

Could this be the kidnappers?

Jake wondered as he watched Rebecca swipe her fingers to unlock the phone, but as she entered her password, he realized that the vibrations were different than a text or an incoming call.

"What is it?" Jake asked. "Another message?"

"No," Rebecca said. "It's the GPS app. It's located Austin!"

Rebecca clicked to open the application, and within a few seconds a map appeared and a large blue circle surrounded central Florida. The screen blinked several times as the map refreshed, each time zooming in closer to Adventure World. It began at thirty thousand feet above and then took a dive into the park. Jake pulled a folded map from his pocket and they laid it out next to the images on the phone.

"Look at this," Jake said, tracing his finger along the wooded area and pond. "Looks just like this area here. Fairy Tale Forest."

"What's the fastest way to get there?"

"There's no easy route, but the quickest way will certainly be if we get on the train." He tapped his finger on the *RR* symbol on the map as Rebecca exhaled a long, slow breath.

"He loves trains," Rebecca said as her eyes welled up. "He was talking about them all morning, asking where they start from and where they end up. I told him that the Olde Railroad Station was near the Prince's Castle, and he took out his map and we identified it together."

"Great," said Jake as he moved close to comfort her. "Let's go."

He took her by the hand and started them in the direction of the railroad. Holding her hand like that, just being with Rebecca, felt so right. But there were so many reasons why he knew the idea of being with Rebecca was wrong.

In high school Jake had thought there could have been something between them. When he'd asked her to the prom, he had hoped she realized he wanted to be more than friends, but by the time he came back from being stationed overseas, she was already engaged to someone else. Jake had thought about telling her the truth about how he felt but could never bring himself to do it. He found it easier to move south and never look back. And now here he was, keeping information from her again. Once she found out that their meeting up today was no coincidence, she might never forgive him.

He could not let his emotions cloud his judgment, especially not now. The last time he was assigned to a kidnapping, he'd allowed his feelings to get in the way, and that had ended in tragedy. Never again.

FOUR

As they approached the entrance of the Dragon's Lair eatery, Jake sensed Rebecca's hand tense up as she slowed down.

"That's a food court. Too crowded. There's no time."

"Trust me," Jake said. "This is the fastest way."

Inside the Dragon's Lair, the crowds were dense and the lines were long. But Jake wove around the snaking queues and offered a polite "excuse us" to everyone they bumped along the way. Just ahead he could see the doors that led to the train station's south entrance, but suddenly he realized there were barricades all along the glass. There was no way through.

"Looks like a dead end. I thought this was a short-cut, but I guess it backfired."

Jake turned his head to look back at the crowds, a sea of people so thick it would be an effort to trudge through that mess again. There was only one way in and one way out. This mistake was going to cost them a lot of time. They were trapped.

Suddenly, Jake saw the man in the red polo enter the café alongside a man in a gray suit. As they spotted Jake and Rebecca, they picked up their pace.

Jake grabbed Rebecca's hand and towed her toward the kitchen counter.

"Come on," he called to her. "There must be another way out."

When they arrived at the silver counter, Jake hopped up and over the top as the young employee at the register yelled at them.

"Hey! You can't go back there."

Jake turned to help Rebecca jump down. "It's an emergency."

They scaled the half wall behind the registers and leaped into the open kitchen area, dodging some of the workers and accidentally knocking over a large tray of French fries. They hugged the side wall and sidestepped the mop bucket before Jake turned and pounded his shoulder into the door. It burst open, just as red polo and his friend touched down in the kitchen. Jake and Rebecca slammed the door closed behind them and pushed a trash dumpster to block it and buy them extra time.

"This way," he called to Rebecca. "And don't look behind us. It will only slow us down."

They hopped a fence into a restricted grass field and raced to the back side of the queue for the train. As they approached, the conductor clasped the lock on the stanchion. The old man wore an engineer's hat and appeared as if he would be perfectly content in his basement racing trains if he didn't have this job at Adventure World. Jake and Rebecca caught his attention as they hopped the fence and cut to the front of the line.

"Excuse us," Jake said. "This is an emergency."

"I'm sorry, sir," the conductor said. "You cannot board. This train is full."

Jake leaned toward the man, pulling his credentials

from his pocket. "I'm an FBI agent. Her son has been kidnapped. Did you hear the Code Adam? People are chasing us, and we need to get to the other side of Adventure World in ten minutes or the kidnappers could do something awful. We need to board."

Jake took Rebecca's hand and started to push through, but the conductor held out an arm to stop them. It was immediately clear to Jake that he was a stickler for the rules.

"Wait just a minute, young man," the conductor said. "I'll have to call this in."

"Every second you waste puts her little boy's life in more danger," Jake whispered.

The conductor slowly lowered his hand to his waist and drew his walkie-talkie from his hip, depressing the button as he raised it to his white handlebar mustache.

"Green Ranger, this is Charlie T. Can I get a confirmation about a Code Adam?"

As soon as he spoke, Rebecca squeezed Jake's arm.

"They could be listening," Rebecca said in Jake's ear. "And I'd rather no one know we're following this GPS signal. We need to take them by surprise."

Jake scanned his eyes along the train and then back at Charlie, who was still awaiting the go-ahead to let them board. Jake motioned for Rebecca's phone and then scrolled to show the threating messages to Charlie T.

"Please get this train moving. We need to be radio silent. If I'm telling the truth, you will be saving a little boy's life. You will be a hero."

Jake could tell that Charlie T. liked that idea, because he nodded toward the train operator and ushered them on.

"All aboard," he called out and pulled on the whistle. Within seconds the train began rolling along the tracks. "Next stop," Charlie T. called out, "Fairy Tale Forest."

Sitting down on the bench seat of the train, Rebecca drew breaths slowly in through her nose and exhaled through her lips. *Smell the brownie. Blow out the candles.* Just as her mother taught her.

Please, God, protect us and guide us. Lead us to find Austin and keep him safe.

When she opened her eyes, she glanced over at Jake and found his eyes were closed as well. Her prayers had truly been answered when he appeared, but she needed to caution herself against feeling so comfortable with him so soon. Could she truly trust Jake, especially after Missy said that Danny had warned her not to trust anyone?

She wanted to ask him why he'd disappeared when he returned home from Afghanistan and if he'd realized how much he'd hurt her. If today had shown her anything, it was that she and Jake had been so close once that they could just pick up where they left off over a decade later. Was there something there between them beginning to take hold? She was trusting him with her life, with her son's life. She needed to believe him.

"Jake," she whispered. "I'm scared. What if they hurt Austin?"

"That's not going to happen," Jake said. "Keeping him safe is the only leverage they have in order to get what they're after. They want that flash drive, and you are the key to recovering it."

Rebecca pulled her phone from her pocket to check the pulsing blue dot on the GPS. Her phone was losing power again, quickly, so she slid her finger to dim the brightness.

"When we are within fifty yards of the GPS tracker, I can make it beep."

"That's fantastic," Jake said, "If they're hiding or we need a distraction, that will come in handy."

As the train pulled into the station, Jake and Rebecca stood and grasped the overhead handrail to steady themselves. They hopped off before they had come to a full stop, much to the dismay of Charlie T., who immediately called it in on his walkie-talkie. But Jake and Rebecca were already on their way, racing straight over to the giant oak tree beside the human-size mushrooms.

Fairy Tale Forest was the oldest section of the park and one of only two areas that remained from when it originally opened in the 1950s. There were small houses where the Three Little Pigs and Hansel and Gretel lived and colorful stone-lined paths through the woods where the kids could pretend to be the Big Bad Wolf or Red Riding Hood making her way to her grandmother's house. At the end of the path, a giant gingerbread man handed out balloons to the children, and Rebecca imagined that it looked and smelled the same today as it had when people her parents' age had come as children, a mix of freshly cut green grass, manicured trees and cedarwood.

As they arrived at the enormous fungi, Rebecca dug her toes into the foot holes in the stems and pushed the button on her phone to make the GPS signal ring out. Her heart raced as she heard the beeping grow louder as she climbed higher, but doubt crept in as she approached the cap.

"Something's not right," she called to Jake. "I hear the tone, but I don't see Austin anywhere."

As she climbed on top of the highest mushroom cap, she saw the bright blue straps and key-chain toys hanging from the zippers. It was Austin's backpack. She jumped down to the lowest caps and ripped it open, bursting into tears when she held the beeping GPS device in her hand.

"It was on his shoe," she said as she silenced the tiny device in her fingers. "They must have taken it off and tossed it in here."

"They wanted to lead us astray," Jake said. "But why?"

Rebecca's heart sank in her chest. Only minutes ago she'd believed she was so close to finding Austin, safe and sound, and now he seemed like he could be a thousand miles away. She knew that with each second that passed, her hopes of finding him alive were fading.

Jake drew a deep breath as he helped Rebecca climb down from the mushrooms. Of course, the kidnappers would identify the GPS tracker and toss it aside at the first opportunity. He knew better and should never have let them waste so much time tracking an empty backpack.

Jake understood that when a child was kidnapped, the first three hours were the most important to finding the victim alive. Seventy-five percent of the kids who didn't make it back to their parents did not survive those first 180 minutes.

Just one year ago, when Jake was on a case, he'd made the mistake of letting his emotions take control, and he went against every protocol to save the boy. And he'd lost him, forever. Since that night Jake had never forgiven himself—and perhaps he never would.

Looking at the desperation in Rebecca's eyes made him doubt himself all over again. Why had Danny chosen him to help her? If only he knew the truth.

But why would these kidnappers have created a distraction? Did they want time to leave the park with Austin? *Where are they now?*

His thoughts were interrupted by a buzzing on Rebecca's phone. She read it quickly before showing him. Another text.

NO POLICE. NO SECURITY. YOU HAVE UNTIL MIDNIGHT TO BRING US THE FLASH DRIVE.

"The timing of that message was no accident," Jake said as he searched all around to see where they could be. "They're watching us and know that we just found the backpack. We need to get off the grid."

Jake scanned the Fairy Tale Forest. They were surrounded by hundreds of families, mothers who skipped along the lollipop paths with their toddlers and fathers who pushed strollers up the long and winding hill to the gumdrop castle. By the lollipop lamps, Jake noticed a few park security guards, but he knew if they were being watched, it was too dangerous to approach them out in the open.

And then he noticed the gingerbread man handing out balloons to the children and waving and dancing in pantomime. Jake grabbed Rebecca's hand and led her into the crowd.

"Excuse me," Jake said as soon as they were close

enough to gain the gingerbread man's attention. "This is an emergency. We need your help."

He gestured to them with his arms open, indicating that he could not speak while he was in character with children within earshot.

"Listen," Jake said, gesturing to his left. "Can you come with us so we can chat? It's a matter of life and death."

The gingerbread man put his hands on his hips, and Jake could see the person inside giving Jake and Rebecca a once-over through the screen in the giant cookie's icing smile. He tapped the heads of the remaining children and waved goodbye before skipping off in the direction of the open fields.

When the gingerbread man was twenty or thirty yards from any children, he broke his silence.

"This better be good," he said. "I can get fired for talking when I'm in costume."

"It's my son," said Rebecca. "He's been kidnapped. Perhaps you heard it called out over the security channels?"

"I don't have a headset in the costume," he said. "But that's terrible. What do you want me to do?"

"I need you to help us get to the underground."

For years Jake had heard the urban legends that Adventure World was actually built on the second floor of the park and there was an entire system of roads and pathways underground. This was part of the original design, modeled after many other theme parks, created to allow the costumed characters to appear and disappear. It also allowed the trash to be collected beneath the surface and for other problems to be swept away out of sight. Jake had been on a tour a few years ago, so he knew that it was true.

"I'm afraid I can't do that, sir. Sorry," said the gingerbread man. "Those tunnels are for employees only. No guests allowed."

"We need to get down there," Jake said. "If you're not going to help me, then I'll find it myself. We could be in grave danger if we spend any more time aboveground."

As they turned to walk away, Rebecca took a parting shot.

"You could be the reason I never see my son again," she said.

The gingerbread man called out to them to return.

"Wait," he said. "Hold on." He scurried ahead to catch up with them. "Let's begin again. I'm Sam."

"And I'm Jake. This is Rebecca. Now are you going to help us?"

"You'll never get down there without one of these RFID chips," Sam said, holding out an ID badge with a radio-frequency identification scanner built in. "And you'll never get in dressed like that."

"Where is the entrance?" Rebecca pleaded. "Come on, we need to move fast."

"A little deeper in Fairy Tale Forest, just north of the Red Riding Hood house. There's a gate beside the house and…oh, come on, I'll just show you."

Sam led them back into the forest and along a candy-covered path toward Red Riding Hood's house. There was a line forming out front, but the three of them moved beyond the house and toward a small picket fence in the backyard.

The sign on the fence said Park Employees Only, and Sam pushed on the gate and opened it slowly. Jake and

Rebecca followed him down a small path that dipped back behind the house. The whole area was an optical illusion, a distortion of forced perspective like something out of the earliest cartoons. From the front of the house, it appeared as if the gate led to a small path that faded into the distance, as the actual road intersected with a painted road on the backdrop of the forest. But in reality the path turned sharply to the left and led down a ramp that went back underneath Red Riding Hood's house. There were two large double doors that would have been impenetrable for Jake and Rebecca, but as soon as Sam scanned his ID card, the doors swung open easily.

"There you go," Sam said. "Now be careful."

"We can't thank you enough," Jake said, as he led Rebecca inside. They had escaped the danger, for now, and were headed down to the secret first level of Adventure World—the underground.

FIVE

Within seconds of entering through the double doors, Rebecca was transported from the mysterious fantasy world of Fairy Tale Forest into an equally enigmatic place set just beneath the house of Little Red Riding Hood. Gone were the deep, lush greens and thatched roofs, and in their place were the cement walls of the industrial corridors that served as the engine for the entire park.

The tunnels were well lit by the large overhead LED tubes running the length of the hallways, and precisely labeled pipes and wire conduits ran along the ceiling and traversed the floors. Adventure World had figured out how to sell millions of sodas, fries and ice cream cones and still sweep the trash away and out of sight, maintaining the utopian illusion for the guests above. And this was how they did it. It made Rebecca cringe to think that everything could disappear so easily. Even a little boy.

As they came to the end of the first hallway, Rebecca was surprised to see the colorful signs above her pointing to a barbershop, a food court and the dressing and costume rooms, with indicators of how far away each was located and also the approximate time it would take in minutes to make it there. Large digital clocks adorned every wall to keep everything running on time.

"I took a tour once," Jake said. "If a character is a moment late to an appearance or photo op, part of the magic disappears. But they can move faster down here to get where they need to go. So can we."

"It's incredible," Rebecca said. "Who would have imagined all this could be underground?"

She smiled at Jake and could not help but notice how being with him made her feel. Since her husband had passed, she had been on exactly one date, and she'd ended it immediately after dinner because she knew it was too soon. But with Jake it felt different. Maybe it was all their history, or his intense focus to help her find Austin from the moment they met again today, but she trusted him and for the first time began to imagine a future with Jake in it.

In high school Jake had worked at the movie theater, and Rebecca, Danny and their friends would use his discount to see every film that came out, sometimes twice. At the end of the night, they would sit in the parking lot for hours and just talk about life. Rebecca remembered that Jake was such a good listener. He was the first person she really talked to about her father and the pain he had caused by leaving them at such a young age. She remembered Jake taking her hand one night and promising that he would always be there if she needed him. This was why it made no sense when he moved to Florida so quickly when he returned home from the marines. But here he was today, right when she needed him the most.

Still, Jake lived in Orlando, and she was still settled in the Northeast. And sure, he was handsome, but they had always thought of each other as just friends. Hadn't they?

You have to let these feelings go.

As they hustled ahead, Rebecca began to feel the burning in her calves again, but she could not dream of resting. Not until they found Austin. She was relieved as they turned the corner and Jake pointed at a row of unoccupied golf carts.

"Perfect," he said as he signaled for her to jump in the passenger seat. Jake felt around under the seat and floor mats before finally discovering the key hidden in the visor.

"Jake, where are we going?"

"That clue from this morning. Didn't it direct you to the Hall of Flags?"

"Yes, but this is not going to be easy. These clues were designed for Austin and filled with facts that only he knows."

"Give yourself credit," Jake said. "You're one of the smartest people I know. You were a straight-A student all through high school. Austin didn't learn everything on his own."

Rebecca smiled, and Jake turned the key just as a voice shouted from behind them.

"Hey, those carts are for authorized security only!"

A tall security guard hustled after them on foot and raised his walkie-talkie to his lips as Jake shifted the cart into gear and stepped on the gas. As they sped away, the guard picked up his speed and called for backup.

"We have two trespassers down here," he said. "Need security. Now!"

Rebecca held on to the handles above her head as

Jake sped up and took the corner on two wheels. They were now in a wider corridor, and up ahead she saw the food court and could not believe how it was nearly as crowded as the restaurants aboveground. Jake pulled the cart over but led her down another corridor and inside the largest costume shop she had ever seen.

From the wall above them, Jake grabbed two laminated cards and handed one to Rebecca. On the face of her card was the picture of the costume of a colonial American woman dressed like Betsy Ross in a flowing blue dress with red and white trim and a white bonnet. Jake's card had the similar layout for a man from that same period. He pointed at the coordinates on the top right hand corner of the card.

"Row H," he said, "section six. We are never going to be able to stay down here unless we make it look like we belong."

The costume room was noisy and filled from floor to ceiling with giant racks of clothing. The entire room was set up on a grid. They proceeded eight rows back until they reached row H, and as they turned down the aisle, Rebecca noticed the large black section numbers painted on the cement floor. Looking up, she realized that the higher shelf held the men's wardrobe while the women's items hung on the first rack. The room was a rainbow of colors, with each land in Adventure World featuring a specific costume. On each rack there were replicas of each blouse and pants in every size. Jake gestured to the dresses and bonnets overhead.

"Find your size," he said. "We need to blend in. Once we are dressed, we can race over to the Hall of Flags in Revolution Square and try to solve that clue."

They stepped into separate changing rooms and Jake

pulled on a puffy white shirt and slipped a pair of blue trousers over his shorts. Rebecca was able to sneak Austin's backpack under her dress and took her sunglasses from her head and tucked them inside. And within minutes, even though they both kept their sneakers on their feet, they instantly looked much less like tourists and more like the Adventure World staff who belonged here.

"My lady," Jake said as he extended his arm. "Let's get ourselves to Revolution Square!"

As they exited the costume shop and made their way back into the underground corridors, Jake was careful to make sure no one was following them. They had managed to avoid the security guards who were chasing them, and he had not seen the two cartel henchmen since before they boarded the train. But he had no doubt they were still in pursuit. Hopefully these disguises could keep them safe for now.

As they walked in the direction of Revolution Square, Jake asked her more about these scavenger hunts that Danny designed.

"So Austin just knows stuff like this? Like the day Florida became a state?"

"He does," Rebecca said. "It's incredible."

"And what was that date again?"

"I have no idea," Rebecca said. "Eighteen forty-something or other."

"It's a good thing we have our phones."

Jake navigated them through the halls until they saw the signs ahead for Colonial Village. He knew that taking these corridors had allowed them to make their way from one side of the park to the other in a third of the time it would have taken if they were aboveground, which was key if they were going to stay one step ahead of the cartel.

As they headed through a small passageway that led to a cement-covered staircase, Jake and Rebecca bounded the steps two at a time until they reached a large blue door. Pulling on the handle brought them back in time to 1776 and ushered them into the Hall of Flags.

"So how does this work?" Jake whispered as they stepped out into the great room that was adorned from floor to ceiling with colorful flags and decorations. "What does Danny leave for him to find? What are we looking for?"

"We will know it when we see it," Rebecca said. "Sometimes there are hidden slips of paper, other times there are small locks or boxes. Obviously it needs to be fairly inconspicuous so the Adventure World staff do not throw it away."

"Makes sense," Jake said. "When did he do all this?"

"He bought a half day ticket for himself yesterday and came in just to set this all up while Austin and I spent the day by the pool. But then something must have gone wrong that forced him to have to get the flash drive off his person at the last minute."

"Someone must have been following him who knew he had the drive," Jake said, "And he figured this was the best way to keep everyone safe."

"He has been very suspicious of people on his team. He did not tell me much, but I know he has been questioning things."

"What else do I need to know about these scavenger hunts?" Jake asked.

"On occasion he will use technology or some other

tools to communicate. He's pretty good with all that stuff."

"Always has been," Jake recalled. "I can't tell you how many times Danny helped me out with my computer back in the day."

Jake and Rebecca moved toward the back wall where the flags were arranged in the order that the states joined the union. He scanned the wall for Florida's flag, which he knew had a red cross with a circle in the center.

"Maybe you should face the crowds," he said, "so it doesn't look like we're tourists?"

"Good idea," Rebecca said, turning around and nodding to some guests with a smile.

The wall was covered with flags, and Jake searched from left to right, top to bottom. But no matter where he looked, he could not see the design that he was looking for, so he took out his phone and did a quick search. Fortunately he had a decent signal, and within moments the information on Florida's state flag began to load.

"What are you doing?" Rebecca said through gritted teeth that remained in a permanent smile. "Someone's coming over!"

Out of the corner of his eye, he noticed as an Adventure World senior staff member dressed as Benjamin Franklin headed in their direction. While many of the employees were in their early twenties, this man did not need a wig to portray a colonist with graying hair. Jake's heart raced as he realized his mistake.

"Pardon me," Franklin said. "But there were no mobile phones in 1776."

Jake swallowed hard as he put his device back in his pocket. He had to think fast.

"A question came up and I do not know the answer,

but we are supposed to be experts. So I tried a quick internet search."

"Aha," said Franklin. "That's why we have break rooms, correct?"

"Absolutely," Jake said. "It's my first time here. It won't happen again."

"Now what was it you were wondering?"

"I need to identify Florida's first flag."

"Well, my lad, for its first forty years, Florida had no flag. The first one featured a white star on a blue background in the top left corner and thirteen red and white stripes," Franklin said, gesturing to the wall. "There were a few other variants before the one that we know today was adopted in 1900 and modified in 1985."

"Thank you so much," Jake said as he backed away from Franklin and moved closer to Rebecca in order to relay the information. But as he approached her, Jake's mind was racing. If there was no flag for those first forty years, then where would he look to find this combination?

"What's going on?" Rebecca asked as Jake drew near.

"I got caught using my phone," Jake said. "We have to remain in character. But we also have to figure out where this next clue is now without the internet. Turns out Florida had no flag when it first became a state. Who knew?"

"Austin would know," she said. "So where do we look now?"

Jake looked around the room for anywhere that looked like a good hiding place. Suddenly he noticed the word *Florida* on a spot on the wall just above a display case. As he approached the case, he noticed a series of photographs inside depicting the early days of Florida's statehood and noticed the date of March 3, 1845, on one of the cards inside. He motioned for Rebecca to join him.

"Is that the date that he mentioned?" Jake asked.

"Yes, I think so," Rebecca said as she bent down and ran her hands up the back side of the case. "Sounds right. I wonder if Danny hid something here?"

Jake crouched beside her and slid his hands under the case. There was a small leg and a lip to the wooden frame, and as his hands moved along the bottom, suddenly he felt the tickle of a folded piece of paper. Jake gave a slight tug, and it fell into his hand. Just then a hand slapped him on the back.

"And what is it that you're doing now?"

Ben Franklin loomed overhead, staring down at him.

"Um, just looking for something," Jake said as he showed him the folded paper. "All set now."

Like an elementary teacher who just caught his student passing a note, Franklin firmly held out his hand.

"Let's see it," he said. "What have you got?"

Not knowing what information the clue contained, Jake was hesitant to comply.

"It's okay," Jake said. "It's just something I found."

"Looks like you found it under the display case," Franklin said. "And since I manage this area, anything found here technically belongs to me."

Jake reluctantly handed him the folded paper and watched as Franklin adjusted his bifocals to read.

"What does this mean?" Franklin asked, his brows raised. "'There is "no way," the apple of your I, this firestorm of the sky...'"

Jake moved behind him to read over his shoulder.

How could he explain this quickly and without arousing further suspicion?

"It's nothing, sir. Really. Just a silly old clue."

"It's intended for me," Rebecca said, swooping in to grab the paper. "And I'd really like it back."

"What are your names?" Franklin asked. "How long have you worked here?"

"It doesn't matter," Rebecca said. "We quit."

She tossed her bonnet at Ben Franklin and grabbed Jake's hand as they raced out of the Hall of Flags and into the middle of Revolution Square.

SIX

Rebecca and Jake dashed across the pavement and climbed the stairs to the blacksmith's shop. From there they cut the line and moved through the exit to the employees-only entrance to the gift shop next door. Inside there were crowds of people and plenty of T-shirts and children's replica costumes on the walls and fitting rooms that provided a perfect place for them to change. Rebecca removed the rest of her colonial garb and rolled the dress neatly into a ball and stuffed it in the corner. Jake stepped out of his changing room and told her he was ready to go.

"So where are we headed?" she asked, pulling her sunglasses over her eyes and slipping her arms into the straps of Austin's backpack as they stepped back outside.

"Let's take a look at that clue again," Jake said.

Rebecca took the paper and unfolded it to read the entire message.

"'There is "no way," the apple of your I, this fire-storm of the sky.'"

"Did Danny always start with such an easy one?" Jake said sarcastically.

"They are easy. For Austin."

"So if we're going to figure this out, we need to think like Austin."

"Easier said than done," Rebecca said. "I've been trying to do that his whole life."

"I'm sorry if that came out wrong," he said.

"No worries," Rebecca said. "I don't take offense easily. But I mean that. It's not easy to understand the way he thinks, but Danny took the time to figure out what videos he was watching and what information he would get most excited about."

"What can you remember? Was there ever something about lightning or fire in the sky?"

"There's a planetarium with a laser show, I think? But that's not even in this park," Rebecca said.

"What about 'the apple of your I'? Or the 'no way.'"

Rebecca thought a moment before her eyes lit up.

"Jose! Austin says, 'No way, Jose' all the time. That has to be a part of it."

"Great. So Jose must fit into it somehow," Jake said. "Do you still have that map? Can you grab it and scan it for the word *Jose*?"

Rebecca unfolded the map and started moving her finger along the top border and also checked the key. She didn't see anything, so she reread the clue.

"Wait," she said. "Austin's been talking about the apple of his eye. It was a few months ago, and it's all he talked about for two weeks. My brother taught him that it meant his favorite thing. His favorite thing is soccer."

"Is there a soccer team with *firestorm* in the name? Or *sky*?" Jake asked.

Rebecca scanned her mind for the names of the cities with professional sports teams. Soccer was her first love, too, having played it in high school, and she had followed the New England women's team before they dissolved. What were the name of the teams? Did any sound like a "firestorm of the sky"?

"What are some of the cities that have professional sports teams? Like basketball, football and hockey?" she asked.

"And baseball?" asked Jake.

"I suppose," Rebecca said, "if you even call that a sport. I hate baseball."

"How can you hate baseball? It's the national pastime."

"The national snooze fest," she said. "Danny takes Austin to the games, not me."

"Ouch," Jake said. "You do remember that I took you to a game once? Our first date."

"First date?" Rebecca said. It had never occurred to her that dragging her to the ballpark was a date in Jake's mind.

"You don't remember," Jake said. "We were sophomores."

"I remember every minute of it," Rebecca said. "We took the Green Line in all the way and got a sausage before *and* after the game. Peppers and onions."

"That's right. I think it went three extra innings."

"Ugh. I remember that, too. Just when I thought it was over, you told me it wouldn't end until someone scored."

"Yup, and then they opened up the field to let fans walk the grounds and you wouldn't stay because we'd already been there so long."

"Don't remind me," she said.

"But I thought you said you didn't remember," he said.

"I remember the game," she said. "I just didn't know it was a date. I mean, you only took me because Danny had his driving test rescheduled for that day. I was just filling in."

From the way Jake looked at her, Rebecca realized that their trip to Fenway Park had meant something more to him than it had to her. Not that she hadn't had a great time being with him that day. Not at all. She remembered it fondly. But she'd always believed she was Danny's annoying twin sister to him, a third wheel.

"I see," said Jake. "You're right. It was just a game."

This was weird. Rebecca's mind started racing as she pieced together other moments in their relationship. He'd taken her to his prom. She'd always figured she was just another person to chip in on the limousine, since Danny took her best friend Suzy and the four of them going together just made sense. But could Jake have been feeling something more this whole time? These were questions they would have to answer later. Right now they had a riddle to solve.

"So for soccer," she said, "there's the New York Thunder, the Philadelphia Spartans, the Los Angeles Strikers, the San Jose Dinos."

"Wait. That must be it!" Jake said. "San Jose and the Dinos. Let's look at that map again."

They opened the map and laid it on top of a recycling barrel. He traced his finger up and to the right corner of the park.

"Dino Land, right there."

"That has to be it," she said. "Austin loves dinosaurs as much as he loves soccer. So we know where we need to go."

"Let's get going. And we can think about 'the fire in the sky' while we move."

As they ran, Jake fired off some clarifying questions.

"So tell me more about these hunts," Jake said. "Do you think we'll find the flash drive in Dino Land?"

"It's hard to know what we'll find. Danny used to take this old toolbox from the garage and put some treasure in it, like a new toy, and then seal it with a hasp lock. And then he'd put all different kinds of locks in the hasp—a three-digit lock, a four-digit lock, a key lock, one with words. Danny would make the combinations the answer to something Austin would know, like the four-digit year that Adventure World opened, or the five-letter last name of the original owners. And he'd hide clues all over the house that Austin would have to find that would lead him to solving the puzzles and then cracking the locks."

"I imagine that Austin liked having it planned out like that."

"He did. It's very important that his day is outlined and that he has a sense of what's coming next. So with something like a scavenger hunt, it's okay if he doesn't know what's coming next as long as he knows it's coming."

"That sounds like a blast. I'm sure Austin loved it."

Rebecca's eyes began to well up thinking about her son. "He did. It brought him so much joy. At first it just took him minutes to solve the locks because his uncle Danny underestimated how much he knew. So Danny made it more complicated, hid the clues in harder spaces and made the combinations harder to crack."

"Let's hope they're not too complicated today."

"Exactly," Rebecca said. "These kidnappers, they mean business. When there's money involved, they will stop at nothing to get back what they want. And I'm afraid we're running out of time."

"Don't worry," said Jake. "We're going to solve this clue and find that flash drive. Then we will rescue Austin and get the cartel off our backs. For good."

Jake feared that Rebecca was right—they were running out of time.

How long before the man in the red polo would find them? The kidnappers had given them until midnight to find this drive, but Jake's instincts told him there was more going on here than met the eye. He wanted so badly to tell Rebecca the truth, the whole truth, about why he was here and what Danny had told him the night before. But not yet. As much as he could not stand keeping this from her, he knew that he was doing this for her safety.

In his head Jake replayed his conversation with Danny from the night before. Danny had had doubts about his partner Lance and suspected that he had gone rogue. That would explain why Danny did not just hand this flash drive over to his superiors if he didn't know whom to trust. So maybe he kept it on his person and then yesterday something happened that led Danny to go back undercover. He couldn't leave the drive in their hotel room, and giving it to Rebecca would put her directly in the line of fire, so he hid it here in the park.

But what was on the flash drive that the cartel and

Lance would possibly want? He was sure Rebecca was right that it probably involved money somehow, but what was on there? Bank accounts? Secrets? Evidence?

Everything in Jake's training was telling him to escalate this and involve the police and FBI. He knew it was dangerous to try and solve this on his own, but those text messages from the kidnappers trumped everything, and Jake couldn't risk Rebecca's or Austin's safety. They had to work alone.

Being here with Rebecca was amazing, and Jake could not shake the feelings that were returning. He hadn't seen her in over twelve years, but it was as if they had not missed a beat since high school. Back then he would hang out with his best friend's sister, and she would help him with his homework while he taught her how to hold the laces to throw a perfect spiral with a football. When they reached the end of their junior year, Jake had asked her to his prom, and they'd had an amazing night. But he was never sure if Rebecca thought of him as more than just a friend. But for the senior year it would be different—he was going to sweep her off her feet. He'd planned the perfect way to ask Rebecca to the big dance again for their senior year. Knowing that she loved those cheesy joke invitations, like spelling "Prom?" with pepperoni on a pizza or writing some ridiculous pun in chalk on the sidewalk outside her house, he made arrangements with her swim coach to sneak into practice so he could submerge a whiteboard sign that she would see as soon as she did a flip turn on her last lap.

But then, just a few days before he could ask her, Corey Salmon hung twenty-five helium balloons in the main hallway of her high school, and when she stepped out of her English class, he stole Jake's thunder. Corey became her prom date, her high school sweetheart and got down on one knee while Jake was overseas in Afghanistan. Austin was born a year later.

And if anything, Rebecca had made it more clear than ever today that the feelings he once had were not reciprocated. He always thought of the Red Sox game as their first date, but it had meant little more to Rebecca than a favor she was doing for her twin brother's friend. And even though she appreciated him being here now, once she found out the truth—that Danny had sent him to watch over her—she might never forgive him.

No matter what he was feeling inside, he had to dismiss it from his mind. He and Rebecca would never be a couple.

When they arrived at the gigantic dinosaur that guarded the front entrance to Dino Land, they passed the small kiddie rides on both sides of the entrance and Jake noticed the incredibly long lines to ride the featured roller coaster, the Comet. One of Adventure World's newest attractions, the Comet was the only ride in Dino Land that was not geared more for the younger visitors.

"Where to?" Jake asked.

"Let's think about that clue again," she said. "'The great fire in the sky, the apple of your I,'" she said.

As she spoke, it became so obvious that he could not believe he had missed it before. The great fire in the sky that some scholars believed ended the age of the dinosaurs. An asteroid.

"It must be the comet. The great fireball in the sky."

A wide smile began to stretch across Rebecca's face. "Of course! Let's go."

As they raced toward the entrance for the Comet, Jake scanned the area for any signs of where Danny could have hidden the prize. If they were going to find that flash drive, they had to move quickly and avoid danger. Rebecca held her water bottle to her lips and emptied the last drop.

"Jake, can you hang onto this backpack? I just need to fill up."

"Sure thing. I'll get in line," Jake said as he took the small pack from her and loosened the straps. He was not thrilled about splitting up, but the filling station was just a hundred yards away and he could keep her in his line of sight. Overhead the Comet dropped from the highest point on the ride, and the guests screamed with excitement. The line inched forward as up ahead, at a point beyond where Jake could see, another group boarded the ride. Within seconds the crowds filled in behind him as he made his way through the queue. Dino Land was so crowded today, and the lines to the Comet were densely packed. Jake adjusted the straps on his shoulder and checked the time on his wrist.

Suddenly, Jake felt the muzzle of the gun press into his lower back and a voice whisper in his ear.

"Walk with me."

SEVEN

As Rebecca waited to fill her water bottle, she marveled at the immense crowds that filled this older section of Adventure World. This was Austin's favorite part of the park when they'd visited years ago, with the life-size dinosaurs for climbing and the sandbox digging pits where toddlers could be entertained for hours. And now with the Comet ride and a similarly titled movie premiering next summer, this had become a must-see destination for every patron. And Adventure World had not missed this opportunity to cross-promote, as the movie posters were painted on every wooden fence surrounding the coaster, images of cities from around the world burning up as the comet crashed to earth.

Rebecca checked her watch. It had been over an hour since the kidnappers last made contact. If she could find the lockbox and recover the flash drive, then this could all come to an end very soon. But even if the Comet was the correct place to begin her search, where would she find it? She had faith that God would guide her, but what if her instincts were wrong?

As she filled the bottle, Rebecca scanned the roller coaster and the adjacent area for anything out of the ordinary. Dino Land was surrounded on all sides by thickly wooded areas, and Danny could easily have hidden the next clue there. But it was unlikely that he would have made them search the entire grounds.

Just then she noticed a small playground up ahead at the bottom of the hill, filled with climbing structures in the shape of the bones of a triceratops, Austin's favorite dinosaur. There were oversize letters spelling out the word *triceratops*, and there must have been at least twenty children climbing and bouncing on them. Rebecca secured the cap on her water bottle and unfolded the clue she had tucked away in her pocket.

There is 'no way,' the apple of your I, this firestorm of the sky.

She screwed the cap back on the bottle and sprinted toward the dinosaur. *The apple of your I.* This had to be it. Danny had hid the clue somewhere near the letter *I* in the word *triceratops*, Austin's favorite.

She glanced over at the line to signal to Jake, but he must have moved ahead. There was no time to waste, so she decided to find the drive now and grab him later.

As she stepped into the play area, she recognized that the giant uppercase letter *T* had a built-in slide and there were three children on it, two climbing up the wrong way and one trying to come down. Their parents were so distracted on their phones that they would not have even noticed if their kids were in danger. Rebecca had been guilty of this a few times herself, but with Austin she had learned that she could not take her eyes off him for even one second. Her body tensed a bit as she thought of him now, missing. She prayed that he was okay and found the strength to keep going.

The uppercase letter *R* was attached to the *T* and was a bouncy bridge to the slide that no one appeared to be on at the moment. Next to that was a letter *I*, which Rebecca noticed was a platform where the children could stand to reach the monkey bars. She looked around and saw that no one was watching her as she climbed up onto the platform herself. She searched for anything that looked like an apple, or a core, or something resembling an answer to this puzzle.

In her mind she replayed the clue. *The apple of your I.* But Rebecca found nothing.

She hopped down and turned back toward the roller coaster in dismay. *Hopefully Jake is having more success*, she thought. She glanced at her phone to see if there was any word from him or anyone else, fearing that if they didn't find this drive soon, she might never see her son again.

Rebecca was surprised at what she saw on her device. This was not a typical text message, but instead there was a red number 2 on top of another application, one that she did not even remember having installed on her phone.

She checked the messages. The first one was from 11:00 a.m. exactly. Rebecca remembered that her phone had buzzed when she and Austin were on the Screaming Serpent, just before her phone had died. And this one was from moments ago. Where was Danny? She couldn't call him when he was undercover. But somehow he was still able to communicate with her?

She read the first message.

Hey buddy. You've made it to the Serpent now and hopefully found the first clue. Love, UD

And then the second.

Good try, buddy. But keep looking for that lowercase i.

Rebecca spun around. It was as if Danny was watching her and knew that she'd just tried to find the clue in the *I* in Triceratops. But if he was watching, why was he still talking to Austin? And if he wasn't watching, how did this text come in at exactly the right time?

Suddenly Rebecca realized how Danny was using the technology in her phone. The first message had been set to come through at an exact time, based upon when their quick-lane Screaming Serpent ride was scheduled. This new message had popped up when she reached specific coordinates, in case they were off course. He had done something like this last month in their local park. Rebecca now realized this was a trial run. He used GPS locations to provide messages to Austin in between the clues, to keep him on the right path. Rebecca smiled. Time to find that lowercase *i*.

Rebecca turned her back to the playground and headed toward the ride when she noticed the movie poster artwork all along the wooden frame of the roller coaster. She had seen the movie trailers, and the premise of the upcoming film was what would happen if a comet, like the asteroid that destroyed the dinosaurs, returned to destroy the planet. Only this time, instead of ending the dinosaurs, it brought them back. Based in science? Not quite. But a surefire summer blockbuster if she had ever heard one.

On every wooden panel there was the name of a city from around the world, each one burning in destruction: Tokyo, London, Paris. This was another brilliant move by Adventure World to give every guest a small sense of home and to welcome people from around the globe. She scanned the panels. Los Angeles, Austin, Boston, Detroit, Chicago, New York. And then it clicked for her. *The apple of* your *I.*

Rebecca broke into a full sprint toward the panel depicting the destruction of Austin, Texas. It was his *i*. The lowercase *i* in his name. The Austin panel was near the back of the ride and was only viewable to those who snaked around the line. She had to climb a small fence to get closer, but there did not seem to be anyone around to question her, and as she approached the wooden frame, she noticed many small bushes and brush on the ground, making for plenty of places to hide something in plain sight. And then she saw it. A metallic apple. The apple of your *I*!

Finally! She reached down and scooped it up in her hands and turned it over to see a four-digit combination lock built in. She knew to try any combination of the date of Florida's statehood, and her fingers shook as she attempted to open it. Rebecca was so excited that she did not notice the figure who had approached her from behind until she felt his powerful hand on her shoulder.

Jake was angry with himself for allowing them to split up. But at least if she wasn't with him, she could still be safe. The man walking behind him and holding the gun to his lower back wore a gray suit and sunglasses, and Jake recognized him as one of the two men who had been chasing them back at the food court. Surely he was sent by the cartel.

"Where are we going?" Jake asked. But the man would not answer. Jake wondered whether there was a language barrier, or perhaps he was just in no mood to talk. The man had moved closer to Jake, and they were walking side by side now in order to appear more natural, but Jake had not forgotten about the Glock in the man's hand. *How could I have been so careless as to let him sneak up on me like that?*

On the case last summer Jake had made a similar mistake. He'd lost his focus for just an instant, but that was enough time for him to learn the hard way that every second mattered.

In that case there was a young child, the grandson of a millionaire, who was being held captive by his mother's boyfriend. Jake knew that so many of these kidnappings were inside jobs—in fact, most abductions were the result of custody disputes and involved a parent. Jake was on the scene with the boy's mother, who slipped away to use the bathroom. She was out of his sight just long enough for the boyfriend to take her hostage and make her his next victim.

After that devastating night, Jake had promised he would never make the same mistake twice, but here he was again, worried about two more people.

Suddenly, the man spoke, but Jake soon realized it was not to him.

"Donde?" the man said into the small earpiece before he stopped short and tapped Jake on the shoulder. He nodded in the direction he wanted them to go.

"Where are you taking me?" Jake asked.

"*Vamos,*" the man said, pointing to the hill on the far side of the attraction. "Let's go."

After about one hundred yards, they stepped over the Danger: No Trespassing sign on the small white fence as they advanced toward the roller coaster. All around them Jake saw the larger-than-life movie posters on the wooden panel fences, each featuring the destruction of one of the great cities of the world. The man led him in between two of the posts between the signs, and now they were out of sight, underneath the ride. The noise was unbearably loud, and it was immediately darker with the shadows from the coaster above looming large. But up ahead he could now see that he was being led in the direction of two figures, the man in a red polo and a woman. It was Rebecca.

Seeing her in danger made Jake instinctively want to reach around his back and grab the man's wrist and make a move to free himself. But with two captors it was too risky, and Rebecca had reported earlier that the man in the red polo had a weapon as well. Jake would have to wait for the right moment.

"Leave her alone," Jake yelled. "She has nothing to do with this. I'm the one you want."

"All we want," said the man in the red polo, "is that flash drive. And she has it."

They were just a few feet apart now, and Rebecca looked Jake in the eyes. She held up something that looked like an apple.

"What is that?" Jake asked.

"It's the lockbox," Rebecca said. "What we've been looking for."

"And now she's going to open it," the man said. "And we will be done with you."

Jake tensed his arms and clenched his fists. He did not care that they had guns—if they did anything to hurt Rebecca, he would take them both down with his bare hands if he had to.

"Open it," the man in the red polo said, pointing his gun in the direction of the lockbox.

"What's the combination?" the man in the gray suit asked.

Jake watched as Rebecca fumbled with the numbers on the dial. She entered 1-8-4-5. The year Florida entered the union. She pulled on the lock. Nothing.

"That's not it," the man in the red polo said, the anger in his voice mirroring the frustration on his face.

Rebecca tried again with a different set of numbers. After three attempts it was clear she was grasping at straws.

"Forget about this," the man in the gray suit said. "Give me that thing."

He took the apple lockbox out of Rebecca's hand and threw it on the ground, hard enough to smash it.

"That's not going to work," red polo said. "We have to open this lock."

"I'll shoot it open." He raised his gun and pointed it at the metal apple on the ground, but the man in the red polo put his large hand out and redirected the muzzle.

"And risk damaging the flash drive inside? Hector will have our heads if we do that."

Hector? Jake's mind raced. Could he be referring to Hector Velázquez, from the Velázquez cartel?

The man in the red polo returned his weapon to his waistband and grabbed the lockbox. With both men facing away from Rebecca and only one of their captors armed, Jake realized this was his best chance.

He leaped forward and reached for the right arm of the man in the gray suit and twisted it forward and into his leg. The gun went off, and the man in the red polo jumped to avoid being shot. As the roller coaster passed overhead, it drowned out everything, and in the ruckus Jake twisted the man's wrist and the gun fell to the ground. Jake kicked up and into the chest of the man in red, and as he doubled over, Jake hit him in the throat while Rebecca rushed in and grabbed the gun that had fallen to the ground.

Jake reached for the other gun in the man's waist-band and held it on them.

"Hands up," he said. "Over your heads."

He separated them and proceeded to search them for any other weapons. Finding none, he took their phones and made them sit on the ground, facing away from each other. It was time to get some answers.

Rebecca saw the fierce strength in Jake's eyes as he questioned the men. She could not believe how he kept risking his own life in order to save her and help find her son. God was truly watching over her by sending Jake to protect her.

"Where is Austin?" Jake asked. "Is he safe?"

Neither man answered. Jake cocked the weapon.

"Somebody better start talking," Jake said.

"Who is Austin?" the man in the red polo asked.

"My son," Rebecca yelled. "The boy you kidnapped."

"What would we want with a child?"

"Don't be foolish," Jake said. "She saw you put your arm around him this morning after you broke down the ride."

"The people we work for are only after one thing

and it's whatever is on that flash drive," said the man in the red polo.

"Who is that?" Jake asked. "Who do you work for?"

"Silencio!" the man in the gray suit shouted as a warning to his friend.

"Is it the cartel?" Rebecca asked.

"Hector Velázquez?" Jake asked. "The Velázquez cartel?"

Neither man opened his mouth, but their silence spoke volumes. Rebecca knew a bit about this cartel from the stories Danny had told her in recent years. The tales were gruesome and frightening, and Rebecca could only imagine the details her brother had left out.

"Where is my son?" she pleaded.

"If you give us what's in that apple, we will tell you what you need to know."

"You're in no position to be making deals," Jake said.

"Neither are you," the man in the red polo said. "You may have us, but we have her son. If I don't check in with my boss in five minutes, your time is up."

"What do you mean? We have until midnight."

"Five minutes. If you don't open that box and give us the drive, you will never see your son again."

Rebecca's heart raced as she turned to Jake.

"We need to talk to Austin now. Once we see that he's doing okay, we will read him the riddle. It's the only way we can open it."

"But what about your brother's plan?"

"I don't care what is on that drive and whether it should go to the DEA or the FBI. I just want Austin back."

Jake took the man's phone, handed it to him and instructed him to make the call.

"Video call," Rebecca said. "I want to see everything you're doing." Rebecca watched as it rang a number that appeared as unknown on the screen. The seconds in between each ring filled Rebecca with hope and fear and anticipation.

Finally, someone picked up on the other end. The conversation began in Spanish, but Jake shot the man a look that convinced him to converse in English. The man's voice sounded familiar, but she was not able to place it.

"They want to see the boy," the man in the red polo said. "Show them that he is okay."

Rebecca's heart pounded in her chest. The video connection was not the best and the noise from the roller coaster overhead was deafening, but despite the shaky and blurry image, she could make out that the camera was moving down a hallway. She could tell from the decor that this was one of the Adventure World hotels. As the door opened, she saw the back of a boy sitting on the edge of the bed in front of the television, immersed in a video game. It was Austin.

"It's your mother. She wants to talk to you," the voice said as he held the phone in front of Austin's face.

"Hi, Mom, how are you?" Austin said without looking up from the screen.

Rebecca's eyes filled with tears. He was in his element. He was okay.

"I'm fine, baby," Rebecca said, composing herself. "I miss you. Is that CraftWorld you're playing? What are you building?"

"I'm making maps of all the train stops and rides." He turned the camera to show the screen, and Rebecca recognized his recreations of the entire park. It always amazed her how much he could create in just a few hours, and this was something she had seen him do a thousand times before. She wondered if his captors were just trying to distract him or if they were hoping he would reveal a clue through the game.

"Where are you, baby?" Rebecca asked.

The man on the other end of the line turned the phone away from Austin, and the screen went black. Rebecca gasped. She had gone too far.

"You've seen he is safe," the man in the red polo said. "If you want him to remain that way, I suspect you will give us what we need."

"But I…" Rebecca started to speak but was interrupted by Jake, who motioned her close as they moved out of earshot of the others.

"Rebecca," Jake whispered. "Don't tell them you can't solve this without Austin. That makes you expendable. We can't have that."

"But what are we going to do?" Rebecca asked. "How are we going to figure this out without his brain?"

Jake pointed to the smartphone she was holding in her hand.

"With this."

EIGHT

In the sixty seconds Rebecca had kept the kidnappers on the phone, she had revealed so much that was useful to Jake's understanding of this situation. Not only was he unharmed, but Austin was indoors in a space with electricity, a television and a gaming system. Since it had been only about two hours since Austin had been taken and he seemed to have created a lot in the Craft-World game, Jake surmised that he had been in that room for a while. This meant that the room was likely an Adventure World hotel room, just a short shuttle ride from the park.

Seeing these kidnappers also convinced Jake that this was not the cartel holding Austin captive. They were being much too kind to the boy to be associated with the Velázquez cartel.

But no matter who they were, he knew that even if he and Rebecca had the upper hand for the moment, it was only hanging by a thread. They were useful as long as they could solve this puzzle and open the box. Jake had dealt with enough bad people in this world to know that as soon as they got what they were after, they would have no use for them—or Austin.

"Read me the clues again," Jake said as he looked down at the four-digit lock Rebecca held in her hand. "Maybe there's something there that will help us to open this combination."

Rebecca repeated the clue: "'There is "no way," the apple of your *I*, this firestorm of the sky.'"

Jake thought about the clue for a moment, but nothing made sense.

"Think hard about the four-digit locks. Did you ever play along and try to help solve them?"

"I did," she said. "The four-digit ones were usually dates, like the years of important events, when a president was born or when the Civil War ended. I already tried 1845 for Florida's statehood, and it didn't work. I feel like we're missing a clue."

"So we figured out the 'Jose' part, right? That was the San Jose Dinos that brought us to Dino World."

"Yes," she said. "And then I realized that the *I* in the clue was the *I* in Austin, painted on this panel right over there."

"So that's how you found this apple. Brilliant!" Jake said. "So what if this clue is all about him? What if it's the year of his birth?"

Rebecca didn't even take the time to respond and immediately grabbed the apple from Jake and began entering the numbers. She tried the lock, but it did not budge.

Jake thought about the remainder of the clue. *There is no way.* They had already figured out that it was "Jose."

"What if we tried the numbers that corresponded with the letters for Jose?"

"Worth a shot," she said.

Jake began counting in his head.

"Try ten. J is ten."

Rebecca began scrolling through the numbers.

"Uh-oh," she said. "The digits only go up to nine. Keep thinking."

C-O-M-E-T had too many letters, as did A-P-P-L-E and A-U-S-T-I-N.

"What about where we are? Adventure World. You said earlier that Austin was obsessed with every fact about this park. When did it open? When did the Comet open?"

"I don't know," she said. "But Austin would."

"Did you open it?" the man in the red polo called out. "You're running out of time."

Rebecca turned to Jake. "I wish Austin were here," she said. "His mind is better than the internet."

"Rebecca, read me that clue again. What was that part about a firestorm? That's the one piece we haven't solved." As she reread the clue, Jake typed the words into the search bar.

Jake watched as the page slowly loaded. The Great Firestorm in the Sky, an event that happened in Minnesota in 1894. Instantly Jake felt like this had to be it. He extended his hand and motioned to Rebecca to hand over the lock. His fingers scrolled through the numbers 1-8-9-4. He pushed up on the lock and, to his relief, it opened.

"You got it! What was it?" Rebecca asked.

"Eighteen ninety-four. A great fire in Minnesota."

"Hinckley! Of course! Austin talked about that incessantly for about a year. It started around the time of the wildfires, and he was watching videos online and somehow fell into a rabbit hole and learned all about the great fire."

Jake handed Rebecca the lock and kept the gun pointed

toward the two men on the ground as she slipped the silver hook out of the clasp and opened the ceramic apple. She reached in and retrieved a small, black USB drive and handed it to Jake. But he noticed that something else inside the apple had caught her eye. He stepped closer to her and peered inside to see exactly what Danny had left for them.

It was another clue.

Without revealing to the men on the ground that she was reading, Rebecca opened the paper while it was still inside the apple and read it to herself. *You'll find the next clue where X marks the spots.* If Danny was using this scavenger hunt to lead them to the flash drive, then why were there more clues? But her thoughts were interrupted before she could arrive at an answer.

"The drive. Give it to us," the man in the red polo snapped. "And we'll be on our way."

"You'll get it as soon as I get my son back."

"That is beyond our control," the man said. "We have our orders."

"That's not what you told us. You said if we found the drive, Austin would be returned to us."

"We said the boy would be safe. And that remains true. Now give us the drive—you will get a call in a few hours and you'll be given instructions to come find your boy."

"That was never the deal!" Jake said as he raised the gun in their direction.

Rebecca reached out and gently placed her arm on his lower back.

"Jake," she whispered. "Let's give them what they want. And trust that they will do what is right."

"Trust the cartel?"

"Trust in God," Rebecca said. "I have been praying all morning since Austin disappeared. He brought us together and He helped me find this apple, and now we can give these men what they're after. And soon Austin will be safe."

She remembered Jake's unwavering faith back in high school, and she hoped that he would still find strength in these words. She could tell that Jake was uneasy with this approach, but she truly believed that this was their best move. In that box was another clue, and she needed to get these men out of the way so she and Jake could continue on their hunt.

She handed the drive to Jake and watched him carefully as he moved it around in his palm while weighing their options. As she waited, Rebecca thought about the clue still in the box. In some ways it was so obvious—perhaps too obvious? *X marks the spots*? It must have something to do with Pirate Island. But why the plural? What did Danny mean by *spots*?

"The drive?" the man in the red polo said. "Hand it over."

"Wait," Rebecca said. "We will give it to you. But first, I need to speak to my son again."

"Midnight," the man said. "You will have him back at midnight. But that's only if you let us go now. And no tricks. No calling the police or park security. Just let us go."

Jake turned his head, and Rebecca sensed confusion in his eyes.

"It's okay, Jake," she said. "Let them have it."

"And let them go?"

Rebecca looked at the clue still inside and slowly raised her head and nodded.

Jake motioned to the man in the red polo to slowly rise, and Jake placed the drive on a small rock in between them. The man took a few steps forward, hunched over and retrieved the flash drive.

"Thank you, Mr. Foster," he said.

"How do you know my name?" Jake asked.

But without answering, both men gave Jake a knowing look that sent chills throughout Rebecca's entire body. Jake may have been holding their weapons, but these men took Austin, and now they had the flash drive. They certainly held the upper hand.

Jake watched the man in the red polo and his accomplice in the gray suit walk off down the hill and in the direction of the exit to Dino Land. He followed them with his eyes until they were out of sight, blending in with the thousands of tourists and happy families waiting in line for the next adventure.

He glanced at the quick-lane bracelet around his wrist and wondered if the cartel knew his name from the quick-lane database at Adventure World. The cartel had warned Rebecca to not involve the police or park security, and yet they were letting him, an FBI agent, assist her. They must not have connected those dots yet, but it was only a matter of time. He shuddered as he realized that his presence could soon put Rebecca in even more danger.

"Are you okay?" he asked Rebecca, putting his arm around her shoulder.

"Yes, you? How did you ever get both guns from them?"

"I've had some practice," Jake said, playing with the weapon in his hand. "Nothing I'm particularly proud of. But I've developed skills that come in handy sometimes."

Rebecca leaned in toward him, burying her head in his chest. Jake held her close and tight, knowing that she trusted him. In his mind he imagined kissing her, touching her soft lips to let her know exactly how he felt inside. But he knew that this was not the right moment—not now, not when she was so worried about her son. And he feared that as soon as she learned he had been keeping secrets from her that the trust she was feeling toward him would be broken forever.

He wanted to tell her now that meeting her here today was no coincidence, but how could he just introduce this now after the leap of faith Rebecca had just taken?

Rebecca slowly lifted her head from his shoulder, and as they finally separated from their embrace, Jake's attention moved on to the clue.

"If your brother hid the flash drive there and that was the main prize, why would there be another clue?"

"Exactly," Rebecca said. "Something tells me that it's a decoy. And they're gone now and it bought us some time to figure this out on our own."

"But supposing it is a fake—what if they realize it and then come after us? Or…" Jake caught himself before he said anything more.

"Or hurt Austin? I know, it's all I can think about. But that's why I'm putting all my trust in God right now. All that we can control is following these clues and maybe we will find what's at the end of this game. If the true drive is buried at the end, then we will find it and we can exchange it for Austin once we have it in hand."

"Did you read the clue? Where should we go?"

As Rebecca read from the paper, Jake realized she had already figured out where they would be heading next. They only had until midnight to find what they were looking for, and all signs were clearly pointing them to Pirate Island—Jake's least favorite place in all of Adventure World.

Jake tucked one of the guns into his waistband and handed the other to Rebecca to carry in Austin's knapsack. As she adjusted the straps and threw it over her shoulder, he took her hand and marveled at this beautiful, resilient woman who was somehow holding it all together despite the danger and embracing this mission and the incredible odds against them.

NINE

With skulls, crossbones and realistic life-size wooden ships everywhere, Pirate Island may have been the most inspirational place in all of Adventure World—certainly for anyone below the age of twelve who had read anything by Robert Louis Stevenson. But what bothered Jake had nothing to do with the parrots and treasure maps and chests of gold. It was the crowds.

Jake remembered reading somewhere that Pirate Island, if it were its own city, would be the most densely populated on the planet. There were seven rides, twelve eateries and an outdoor pirate ship playground beloved by toddlers and teenagers alike. And all this was just a short boat ride from Surf City, the water park section of Adventure World adjacent to Dino Land that they were running through as fast as they could possibly move.

Jake felt a burning in his shins, and so he slowed his pace as they approached the dock, allowing him to consider which of the options would get them to Pirate Island the fastest. Would they board the pirate ship and cross the lagoon or walk along the plank, a long wooden bridge connecting the island to the rest of the park?

Jake stared at the incredible crowds shuffling along

in front of them. Either option was going to take more time than they had to spare.

"What are we going to do?" Rebecca asked. "This is packed."

"Follow me," Jake said as an idea struck him. He took her by the hand and raced toward the giant wave pool.

Surf City was a water park within Adventure World, complete with waterslides, a lazy river, tube rides and a splash pool for the youngest visitors. They entered through the main gates, where hundreds of guests were watching the countdown at the wave pool, and sneaked behind a lifeguard chair. When they reached the ramp, they turned left and walked down toward the same system of underground tunnels they had been in before.

As they approached the double doors, Jake pulled on the handle, but they would not budge.

"No worries. Someone will come out any minute," Jake said. "Why don't you grab us those buoys over there? We will blend in more if we look like we work here."

Rebecca reached for the bright orange lifeguard cans and handed one to Jake.

"How do you know about all these tunnels and underground parts of the park, anyway?" she asked. "Was this all a part of that same tour you took under Fairy Tale Forest?"

"Yes. An old friend of mine was obsessed. She believed this was the only way to truly get the full Adventure World experience."

"She?" Rebecca said, raising a brow.

"Yes, she," said Jake. "And like I said, she was an *old* friend. As in ex—"

He wanted to make it clear that he was single, but the truth was Jake and Alyssa had only broken up last summer. They were very serious; in fact, Jake had even bought a ring. But his whole life had unraveled after he had failed to rescue that kidnapped boy. If he couldn't save that child, how could he protect a family of his own? How could he be a husband and a father and live up to all that would be expected of him?

When Jake began doubting himself, he became obsessed with work, and he'd spent most of the past year fixating on the details of where he went wrong. Their breakup was as much his fault as it was hers for finding someone else. And even though Jake realized this now, the truth still stung every time he pictured Alyssa in the arms of another man.

But now, for the first time, Jake realized that there was something more that had caused that relationship—and every other one he had attempted in the past decade—to end. In fact, they'd never had a chance, because none of those women were Rebecca.

"I had been wondering if you'd found anyone," Rebecca said.

"Still single," he said. "No one serious yet. You?"

"I have no time for dating. Since Corey died, I've been one hundred percent engrossed in being the best mom I can be."

"You've done an incredible job."

"Thank you. It's so great finally catching up with you. From the moment I saw you this morning, we've been on the go and haven't had the chance."

"I know. What a day. But it's been amazing, Beck. It's like we picked up right where we left off."

"I know. I can't thank you enough. I'm sorry that we've fallen out of touch. I'm not sure how."

Jake wanted so badly to tell her the truth, the whole truth, right then and there. Would she be shocked to learn she had broken his heart by choosing Corey? And was it so hard to imagine that Danny had asked him to protect her today? The longer he kept these truths from her, the more hurt she would be when she finally discovered the whole story. But she spoke before he had the chance.

"I'm just so glad that you're with me right now. There's no one else I'd rather have helping me."

Jake opened his arms and invited her in for a friendly hug, but as pulled her close this time, he sensed there was something more. Ever since high school, he had imagined what it would be like to kiss her. *Was she feeling this, too?* In that moment there were no crowds, no cartel, no danger. It was just Jake and Rebecca.

Suddenly the doors burst open, and two lifeguards emerged, forcing Jake and Rebecca apart. Jake grabbed the door before it closed again.

"Act like you belong here," Jake whispered, "and no one will question us."

Thankfully, the costume of a Surf City lifeguard was easy to replicate, and they blended in quite easily. With sunglasses and T-shirts, all they needed were these lifeguard props to disguise the fact that they were guests and not Adventure World staff.

The hallway of the tunnel was dimly lit, and it took a moment for Jake's vision to adjust from the bright sun, but soon they were at the end of the first corridor. Jake pointed to the sign above them with an arrow to the left pointing the way to Pirate Island. Jake knew that this tunnel should lead them under the lagoon and right where they needed to be to follow Danny's next clue. But suddenly he heard someone yelling from behind them.

"Detenerlos!" he yelled. "Stop them!"

Looking over his shoulder, Jake glimpsed the men they'd last seen under the Comet roller coaster now about one hundred yards away, running toward them at full speed.

"Run!"

Jake wondered what had gone wrong. Had they figured out that Rebecca had found another clue? Was the flash drive they handed over not the one they wanted?

The tunnel had been empty, but now Jake could see a handful of costumed pirates moving in their direction who started to see all the commotion. Jake reached into his waistband to grab the weapon but decided at the last instant to use the rescue buoy to smash the lights on either side of the corridor, making it just dark enough to slow everyone down.

"Hey, what are you doing?" one of the pirates called out in the darkness.

"Keep moving forward," Jake said to Rebecca. "Don't stop no matter what."

As they passed by the costumed pirates, the tunnel forked in two directions, and Jake smashed the light to the left but led Rebecca to the right.

"What are we doing?" she asked.

"Hold on," Jake said as he led her to the side and they ducked behind an iron column. They waited and watched as red polo came to the intersection and took the darkened path.

"He thinks we went that way," Jake said. "Come on."

They quickly resumed their sprint down the hallway and did not slow down, but as they came around a bend, Jake's sneaker hit a wet spot and he felt his ankle slip beneath him and twist. He hit the ground hard, and Rebecca gasped.

"Are you okay?" she asked.

"I'm fine," he said. "Just keep running."

"I'm not going anywhere without you," she said.

Jake hopped up, and he felt the burn shooting up his leg but knew that he'd lived through much worse. He quickly tightened the laces and they resumed their ascent. He hadn't heard or felt anything pop, so that was good. He knew that stopping now would certainly lead to a more unfortunate alternative than surging ahead.

"There," he said, pointing at the glimmer of natural light up ahead. "Just a little bit more."

Rebecca turned right at the door that led into the stairwell. They were on the bottom level, and so she turned and continued up the steps, taking them two at a time. As she reached the first landing, she stopped for a moment and waited for Jake. The stairs were difficult for him, and she could tell he was in pain.

How had they gone in thirty seconds from a quiet moment where they nearly kissed to being back on the run from the cartel? *And that is what nearly happened, right?* She did not know if these were old feelings coming back to the surface or just the adrenaline from today, but there was no doubt in her mind that when Jake pulled her close there was something there. But more importantly, she knew that she could not let anything distract her from finding her son.

Rebecca pointed at a sign that read, Skeleton's Cove, Level 2. The Shipwreck, Level 3.

"Through here?" Rebecca asked as Jake made his way up the steps.

"One more flight."

Up above she heard the sounds of security guards on walkie-talkies rushing down the stairs toward them, most likely because of their destructive behavior. She looked for a place to hide.

"Over here," Rebecca said, grabbing Jake's hand and leading him behind the stairs to a storage area with large barricades used to block off the roads during the parades. They were just big enough for Rebecca and Jake to sneak behind until they were in the clear.

As the guards rushed down the stairs, Rebecca held her breath. If one of them looked in their direction, they'd be caught. And the guards were the least of their worries. The cartel was back after them, no doubt realizing the drive in the apple was a fake. She had to follow the remaining clues now and find that real drive fast. Their lives depended on it.

With the security guards out of sight, Rebecca knew that the only way for them to be safe again was to head outside and disappear into the crowds. This downtime had not helped Jake's ankle, and his limp was more pronounced as they climbed the stairs to the top of the level-three landing. Rebecca pushed on the doors, and they once again found themselves in the bright sunshine. There was an immediate, almost deafening, change in the volume, as if they had moved from an empty church on a weeknight into a packed football stadium after a touchdown.

Once they were outside, they raced into the giant

shipwreck attraction in order to blend in with the hundreds of guests exploring the grounds. Jake winced with every step, but Rebecca pushed them farther into the crowd until she felt they were in the clear.

"We need to find you a first aid station for your ankle."

"I'll be fine."

"Jake, I need you at one hundred percent. I can't do this without you."

"Don't worry about that," he said. "I can shake this off. Trust me. We don't have a moment to waste. The cartel does not mess around."

As they approached the shipwreck, Rebecca marveled at the spectacle they were entering, a ship split in half with the bow pointing up at the sky revealing a cross section of the pirate vessel for the children to explore. Nearly everyone in sight had a patch over one eye and a tricorner hat and a plastic swashbuckling sword.

"So have you been here before?" he asked.

"Once, years ago, when Austin was very small. Too young to remember."

"Do you have any more thoughts about that clue? 'X marks the spot'?"

"Spots," she reminded him.

"Right, the plural. That was the confusing part. There's a ride where the kids are given a treasure map, right? And they have to follow the maze and find all of the markers and come out on the other side. Maybe there are multiple spots on that map?"

"The Sunken Treasure," Rebecca said pointing west. "Just over there on the other side of the pirate ship playground."

Rebecca remembered the Sunken Treasure and how

Austin, at three, had taken off into the maze and it took them nearly twenty minutes to find him that day. It had been one of the most terrifying moments of her life, and even now, so many years later, she had refused to take him anywhere near this attraction. Danny knew this well, and so he would not have led them there. And it was too obvious to be the place where "X marks the spots."

"But I don't think that's where we need to go," she said. "It's too on the nose for Danny's game." She thought for a moment before making her way to a large painted map on the back of a wooden sign. She studied Pirate Island, searching for clues.

"Where could he want us to look?" Jake asked.

Rebecca traced her eyes all across the map and stopped when she came to place labeled Quick Pixx. She looked up to see the actual location—the photo booth at the bottom of the pirate coaster where guests could purchase the photos snapped by Adventure World cameras as they took the final plunge. As she looked back at the map, she tapped her finger on the double letters in the word *Pixx*.

"This is it," she said. "It's the spot. Or spots. This is where the drive must be buried."

Jake trusted Rebecca's instincts about this clue, since she had played Danny's games before. But as they moved through the crowds in the direction of the photo booth, Jake still had a thousand questions.

"How do you reach your brother when he's undercover? Is there any way to contact him?"

"When he's deep under, no," she said. "Sometimes he

doesn't even tell us where he's going. I usually reach out to the people on his team, like Missy, one of his partners back in Boston."

"Have you been in touch with her today?"

"I haven't tried yet," Rebecca said. "She is the one who called me last night. And she knows we're here. Missy is the one who suggested we go to Adventure World to get away and take some time to relax. Danny wasn't interested at first. But then all of a sudden he was convinced we should make the trip."

This all sounded strange to Jake. It was too convenient that Missy would suggest they take this trip and now Danny was missing in action and the cartel was after Rebecca. He wondered what Rebecca knew of Danny's doubts about his partner Lance, but he feared that the more he pressed her, the greater the chance that he would let on that he had spoken with Danny just last night. He had promised not to tell Rebecca about their conversation, and although he did not like having to choose between a promise to his best friend and betraying the trust he was trying to build with Rebecca, for now he had to keep focused on the task in front of them.

"Okay," Jake said. "Maybe after we find this next clue, we will get a message to Missy that she can send to Danny. We need to tell him what's happened today."

Rebecca nodded, and Jake smiled, but in his heart he knew that Danny's cover was already blown. If the cartel had deduced that the drive was stolen that quickly and knew enough to come to the park and follow Rebecca, then they certainly must have figured out his identity and known that he was DEA. Jake winced as the image entered his mind of Danny paying the ultimate price for his deception—followed by the realization that Rebecca's life was clearly in more danger now that the cartel was back on their trail.

TEN

The massive Jolly Roger flag flying above the Quick Pixx booth confirmed the feeling Rebecca had that this was the place her brother had chosen to bury the prize they were seeking. She knew they needed to act fast and find that drive before the men caught up to them again.

Of course, if they did, Jake would protect her. She was so thankful for him and could not stop thinking about the kiss they'd nearly shared. The moment had been so perfect and natural, but was it real? Or were they just caught up in the moment?

Within seconds Rebecca chastised herself for thinking of anything other than escaping this mess and saving Austin.

When they arrived at the Quick Pixx booth, she signaled to Jake to split up and move around the perimeter of the building to search. It was small enough that they could begin to look for any X that marked a spot, or anything that appeared slightly out of place.

"Look for a rock," she said, "or a potted plant that just doesn't look right."

"But Danny needed the clues to still be here when you guys arrived, right? Couldn't a flower pot be moved?"

"True. But he only set this up yesterday. I think it's going to be buried a bit. He's done an 'X marks the spot' clue before and buried the treasure under a plant in the garden about six inches deep in a small box."

Jake nodded and then headed to the left around the building while Rebecca circled to the right. She approached the trash barrel and recycling container and gave them a slight nudge. But they were too heavy to move, and there did not appear to be anything nearby on the ground that looked as if it had been recently displaced.

As she made her way to the back of the building, she noticed a large row of tight bushes and trees that were up against a half wall. Behind the wall was a significant drop to the winding path below. This was not a good cut-through for any guests, and so the only people who ever came back here were those who worked in the photo booth. The perfect hiding spot.

Along the back outside wall of the building, Rebecca spied a small brick walkway leading to the back door. The Dutch doors were split open, with the solid bottom closed but the top wide-open. All that stood between Rebecca and the Quick Pixx employees inside was a screen to keep out the mosquitoes. She would have to stay quiet to avoid detection, as this was a place where she surely did not belong.

The red bricks on the walkway were all raised slightly from years of tree roots expanding underground, and there was a small stone wall along the tree side of the walkway, but she did not find an X or any indication of where the next clue might be hidden. And then Jake called out to her.

"Psst. I think I found something."

Rebecca crouched down as if playing leapfrog and shuffled her feet in his direction. She was very careful to keep her head below the opened top of the Dutch door, but just as soon as she stepped off the bricks and onto the dirt, she heard a voice call out from inside the photo booth.

"Hey, you. What are you doing back here?"

Rebecca turned around slowly, searching for the words. The woman who stood there was older than many of the other park employees and wore her graying hair in a bun on top of her head, her black-rimmed glasses hanging on a chain around her neck.

Rebecca needed to think fast.

"My brother lost something," Rebecca said, pointing to the ride above her head. "It fell down here, I think."

"Was it a hat? Or a phone? People are dropping things from the coaster all the time. They need to read the directions and take it seriously when they say to secure your valuables."

As they moved around to the corner of the building, the woman noticed Jake, his fingernails covered in dirt, kneeling over a small hole in the ground. She squinted her eyes and glared at Rebecca.

"Things that drop from the coaster don't bury themselves that deep in the ground. What are you two up to?"

Jake tapped his fingers on the top edge of what sounded like a metal box. "I know this is strange, but I noticed a brick that looked out of place, and I've found something buried here that we've been looking for all day."

"Stop what you're doing," said the woman. She whispered into her walkie-talkie and alerted park security.

"Standard protocol for whenever we find something like this. Could be an explosive. Could be anything."

"It's not an explosive," said Rebecca. "It's a part of a scavenger hunt. My brother buried it for me to find, as a clue."

"Well, we'll just see about that," said the woman.

Jake rose slowly from the ground and approached Rebecca to whisper, "She's just doing her job. But we don't have time to waste. Should I pull rank and flash a badge?"

"We need to find out what's in that box," Rebecca said through clenched teeth. "And if they are thinking that this could be a…well, then they're not going to let us open it."

Rebecca stepped forward and moved toward the box that was buried in the ground. Suddenly she felt the phone in her pocket vibrate.

"Miss," the woman said, "I'm going to ask you again to step back away from that box."

Rebecca stepped back and looked down at the message on her phone. As soon as she read the screen, she grabbed Jake by the arm.

"We're going to take a little walk. Just over to that bench until someone arrives."

"What is it?" he asked as soon as they were out of earshot.

"It's a geo-location message. From Danny."

Jake knew enough about the technology to understand that Danny had entered some coordinates into her phone so that as soon as she was near the clue, it would send her a message. But this was a brilliant way for him to communicate with her now at the park, like a digitized game of hot and cold.

When they sat on the bench, Rebecca nodded and handed him the phone so that he could read the message on the screen.

Beck, to watch my message, search for your favorite place and color. The password is your imaginary friend.

Make sure you're alone.

"Do you know what he's talking about? How to find this video?"

"I think so," she said as he passed her the phone. She opened up the video player and searched her favorite place and color. When she clicked on the link it asked for a password, and she entered the name of her imaginary friend.

"Do you want to be alone?" Jake asked.

Rebecca looked at Jake, closed her eyes and shook her head. If Danny knew that Jake was here with her, he would trust him with whatever it was he had to share. She grasped his hand and interlocked their fingers.

"This is it. Let's watch."

Within moments the video began to play. It was hard to hear, so Rebecca adjusted the volume to the maximum, and they tilted their heads to get as close as possible to the speakers.

Out of the corner of his eye, Jake watched as Danny's face appeared on the screen. Perhaps more now than ever he looked to be Rebecca's twin—the same blue eyes and dimples in the cheeks. But Danny had the scruffy stubble of a beard with just the slightest hints of gray that made him look older. He held the camera in a low angle at an extreme close-up, like so many of the online vloggers did. But unlike those influencers, Danny's tone was deadly serious.

"Beck," Danny said directly into the camera. "If you're watching this, that means you found the clues and you and Austin are doing the scavenger hunt. What you need to know is that it's critical that you play along until you find the prize at the end."

Jake watched Rebecca's eyes as they were filling with tears at the sight of her brother, who continued to speak with a hint of desperation in his voice. Danny held the camera a bit farther back from his face. In his hand he was holding something small and shiny. It looked like a key.

"This is a flash drive," he said. "I've kept it on my key chain since I recovered this data a few weeks ago after the raid. It contains a map with the location of several stolen paintings from that heist in Boston back in the early '90s. The artwork that was taken is worth millions, and there are some very bad people who are tracking this down. Once you recover it, you need to immediately take it to the FBI. There's a reward for the recovery of the artwork, which will help pay off your debts and get Austin everything he needs."

Rebecca turned to Jake. "I don't understand. Why didn't he just give it to me? And why didn't he turn it in to the FBI himself?"

Danny, on the video clip, continued, "They're after me, Beck. Someone knows that I have this, and they will stop at nothing to get it back. I could not think of any-where to hide it, and I've lost trust in everyone. Except you. And Austin. So I'm going to disappear for a while now, but if you follow the clues, you will find the map. Make sure you bring it to the FBI, Beck. Follow all the clues. And do not trust anyone."

In the video, Danny looked to the left and the right as if he were checking to make sure no one was looking before he concluded, "Love you. Take good care of my little buddy."

The screen turned black, and Rebecca lowered the phone. It was as if these last words from her brother were his final goodbye to her, and she began to sob. As Jake held her close, he knew that she was feeling everything—the fear of what could happen to Austin, the heat, the exhaustion and the confusion as to whether Danny was dead or alive.

Danny looked terrified in that video. Desperate. If the cartel knew he had stolen from them, then it was clearly within the realm of possibility that he was dead.

But it was the last words Danny spoke that bothered him the most. Telling Rebecca to "not trust anyone" could make her begin to question their coincidental reunion today, the way he turned up at exactly the moment when her son went missing. He knew he needed to tell her the truth soon if she was ever going to fully trust him.

But Jake was jarred back to attention as the woman from the photo booth called out to them. She stood next to a park security guard who was holding the metal box in his hands.

"Looks like there's some sort of riddle or clue on the back of this," he said as they approached. "Do you mind telling me why you were digging beside this booth on Adventure Land property for a locked box?"

Rebecca looked to Jake for approval before continuing.

"Sir," she said. "I'm the mother whose son has been kidnapped. I'm Rebecca Salmon. The kidnappers told us never to talk to security or police, but we did make an initial report that he was missing. Maybe someone has told you about us?"

The security guard nodded. "The Code Adam. Right. I've been informed about this. You two went missing after someone dressed as a security guard attacked you backstage."

"So you see why we are having trouble trusting anyone at Adventure World after that," Jake said.

The security guard nodded but still appeared confused, and so Rebecca continued.

"The kidnappers are listening to your radio communications. They're probably on their way here now. They want what's in this box and will stop at nothing to get it. They told me if I went to the police or to park security, they would hurt my son," Rebecca said. "So even now, right now, I'm putting his life in danger by talking with you."

The guard squinted his eyes and stared at her.

"So what's in the box?"

"It's a scavenger hunt," Jake said. "A wild goose chase. We need to follow the clues to get the bad guys what they want or else…"

"Or else what?" the guard asked.

"They have my son," Rebecca said. "Are you going to make me say the words?"

The guard looked Rebecca and Jake over and then looked back down at the box and its three-digit lock.

"So how will you open it?" the guard asked. "What's the combination?"

"This is the tricky part," she said. "Without my son here, this is more challenging to figure out."

"Can you give us the box," Jake asked, "so we can try?"

"No way," said the guard. "I'll hold on to it, and if you give me the combination, I will try it."

Jake looked to Rebecca for a guess.

"Any idea what it could be?"

"Three-digit codes are usually a combination of things. Sometimes it's a birthday, a day and month. Other times it could be my age and Austin's age, in some order."

"Should we try that?" Jake asked.

"But didn't you say there was a clue on the box?" Rebecca asked.

"Yes, a riddle," the guard said, and he turned the silver box over to reveal the scribbles in red near the bottom hinge.

Jake moved closer to read what was inscribed on the box in permanent marker.

It will not help you dig, but if you see it you will die.

Jake racked his brain but could not think of anything that would give him a hint about the clue. The woman from the photo booth weighed in.

"The only thing I can think of is a shovel," she said.

"No, Emma," the guard said. "It says that it will *not* help you dig."

"What about the second part of the clue?" Jake asked. "'If you see it you will die'?"

"What is it that if you look at it you die? Some kind of mirror or something?" Emma asked.

"No," the guard said. "That will turn you to stone, I think."

"But there is something," Jake asked. "I think I remember a song about it."

"Think of our surroundings," Rebecca said. "Pirate Island. Don't they give each other the black spot as a sign that they are a traitor?"

Emma looked at the box. "So should we try 'spot'? Are we looking for numbers or letters?"

"Three numbers," Jake said. "And so *spot* has too many. It's also too low in the alphabet. Those dials probably only go up to nine, right?"

The guard looked at the box and spun the dials. He nodded.

"Yup, nine."

Jake could see everyone searching for an answer. Finally, Emma's eyes lit up, and Jake could tell that she'd had a revelation.

"I've got it," she said. "Ace. The ace of spades is what they used to give pirates in the Caribbean. It's the inspiration for the black spot."

She turned to Rebecca. "I used to give the boat tour of Skeleton's Cove, and it was one of the fun facts I shared with the guests."

"Brilliant," said Jake. "And a spade could be used to dig, but not a playing card spade. Try one, three, five for the combination."

The guard took the box and turned it over and entered the numbers, lining the dials up to the corresponding combination that Jake had just requested. As he was about to attempt to slide the locked box open, he hesitated, looking at Emma.

"What if we open this and it triggers something to detonate?"

"I'm telling you the truth," Rebecca interrupted.

"This is a game for my son to solve. There is nothing dangerous about opening that box. The only danger is in all the time we are wasting not getting to that next clue."

Emma nodded her approval, and Jake recognized that there was just something about Rebecca that made people believe her. She was a mother searching for her lost child who was emanating this sincerity, this passion, and it made people want to break ranks and go against their instincts just to give her any support that she needed.

The guard pushed the switch to the side, and the clasp on the lockbox flipped open. He slid his thumbs up to the lid and pushed open the box.

Everyone was shocked to see what was inside.

ELEVEN

Rebecca could see clearly now that in the box there was a very expensive-looking car key on a fancy embroidered key ring. The guard lifted the ring from the box, holding it between his index and forefinger, and Rebecca counted four keys.

One was clearly to a vehicle. The next one looked like a house key. The third one was smaller and round, like for a shed or a lock. But the fourth key was the one that looked the most familiar. In fact, Rebecca knew it was not a key at all.

Much like her brother had intended, everyone was so distracted by the very flashy car key that they did not notice the key-shaped flash drive that Danny had hidden in plain sight.

Rebecca sneaked forward a step or two and stole a glance into the box to see if there was anything else inside.

"What's that?" she asked.

Emma reached into the box and removed three four-by-six-inch photographs. She studied them each for a moment with a puzzled look on her face before turning them over to Rebecca.

"Beats me," she said. "These look like a hotel lobby? And a bus? And what's this one?"

Rebecca took the images in her hand and flipped through them as Jake approached to look over her shoulder. She recognized the hotel lobby as the one where she was staying, the Adventure World Grand Hotel. The bus was also instantly familiar, as it was one of the air-conditioned buses that she and Austin took to come to the park from the hotel. But the third photo was unclear. What was it?

"Is that a strawberry?" Jake asked, leaning in. "Like in extreme close-up?"

"It's a screen," Rebecca said, realizing it herself as she explained. "It's a terrible photo taken through a screen. The flash went off, so all you see is the screen."

"Why would someone include that?" the guard asked. "That's one you usually just delete, not print."

"We will have to figure that out," Jake said. "Thank you both for all of your help."

As they turned to walk away, the guard held out a hand to restrict their movement.

"Please," Rebecca said. "You need to let us go. We are being followed, and they'll be here any minute. And you need to stay off the walkie-talkies about this. They're watching us and listening to every move."

The guard looked to Emma and then back to Rebecca.

"I'm sorry," he said. "I can't promise you that. There is a standard response to a kidnapping at Adventure World, and I can tell you that this place is already swarming with security who are looking for you. But what I will do is hand deliver this box to my supervisor and not call it in. And as for what's inside, I'll pretend I never saw it.

It may cost me my job, but if what you're saying is true, then letting you get out of here now might save some-one's life. But once this box is in my supervisor's hands, it will be up to him, and I can't guarantee anything."

Rebecca looked to Jake, who nodded. It was the best offer they were going to get.

"Thank you," she said. "A million times over. God is guiding me here, and He brought us to you. We never would have solved this without you." She hugged Emma and the guard before turning to Jake to begin the next leg of their journey.

"Where are you heading?" they asked.

"The buses," Rebecca said. "We need to go back to the hotel."

"Come on," the guard said. "I'm going to use my boat to go back to the headquarters. I'll give you a lift."

It turned out there was a fourth way off the island and this was in fact the fastest. The guard's small mo-torized boat zipped along the water and brought them back to the mainland of Adventure World in no time. When they arrived at the shore, Jake helped Rebecca off the boat, and they thanked the guard again for his help.

When they were alone, Jake warned Rebecca that things were about to change.

"He's to tell his boss now," Jake said. "About everything. They're going to put two and two together and realize we're the ones who were sneaking around in the tunnels, smashing out the lights. They're going to call this one in, Rebecca. I guarantee it."

Rebecca knew that he was right. They'd given every-thing they had to solve this mystery, and now that she had this key-shaped flash drive, she felt like she was get-ting closer. But despite all their efforts in solving Dan-

ny's clues, she realized that she was no closer to having
her son by her side. But at least she had something to
trade for him if she came face-to-face with the cartel.
With every second that the clock ticked closer to midnight, she knew that their lives depended on it.

They were walking briskly now, retreating back
through Surf City and up over the hill that led back toward the main gates. Jake wondered about those three
photographs and the fancy keys that he now held in
his hand.

"What about the car?" he asked. "Any ideas? Would
Danny have rented something like this? Maybe it's a
sports car?"

"No clue," she said. "We took a shuttle from the air-
port, and Danny never mentioned that he was renting
a car. I wonder where it's parked? Back at the hotel?"

"What about the other two photos?" he asked.

"Definitely the hotel lobby," she said. "I recognized
the giant train set in the corner of the photograph.
And of course Austin was obsessed with it when we
checked in. It took me almost half an hour to get him
upstairs that first night. It was so bad I've taken him
out through the side doors ever since to avoid him getting distracted."

"And what about the third one?" he asked. "The one
with the screen and bad flash?"

"I have no idea on that one, either," she said. "We're
going to have to figure that out ourselves."

As she looked at the photos, Jake noticed something
on the back of one. In red letters, Jake read, "13W."

"What's that?" he asked, prompting Rebecca to
turn the photo over to see it herself. She had the pho-

tos stacked and the photo with the writing on it was the one of the bus.

"Thirteen W," she said. "Could that be seat 13W? On the bus?"

"There's only one way to find out," Jake said.

As they exited the park, Jake began to wonder about whether he would set off the metal detectors but noticed that they would not be going through them again as they exited. He then remembered his own gun, checked in at the front gate.

"Rebecca, I need two seconds to grab something."

Jake ducked into the security station and was relieved that there were only two people ahead of him in line. Time was not something they had to waste. As the line moved forward, Jake stepped up and fished in his pocket for his identification. Just then, out of the corner of his eye, he saw the security guard from Pirate Island speaking to his supervisor in the corner office.

Rebecca and he had taken a different route back to the security checkpoint, but the guard from Pirate Island had been heading to the same destination. Their interactions to this point had been friendly and supportive, but something told Jake that if the guard witnessed Jake being handed his gun, he would question why Jake had failed to mention that he was an FBI agent. That was not a conversation Jake was looking to engage in, and since he already had the gun in his pocket that he'd recovered from the man in the red polo shirt, he decided to step out of the line and move quickly to catch the next bus to the hotel.

Getting through the exit of Adventure World appeared to be no easy task. Since they knew both security and the cartel could be looking for them, they slipped into the gift shop and bought an enormous stuffed Worldy doll, the Adventure World mascot, and some hats and glasses that would serve as a disguise through the gates. Jake suggested that they exit separately and each sidle up to another family and then rendezvous by the bus stop in five minutes. He knew it was dangerous to separate, but he had to trust his instincts if they were going to solve this next clue—one that lay outside the gates of Adventure World.

As she arrived at the bus stop, Rebecca smiled as she imagined the enthusiasm Austin would have felt at seeing the long line of people queued up for the ride. Thinking of him caused her eyes to well up and her lower lip to quiver. She took off the hat and glasses and tucked them into her backpack and left the Worldy doll, which her son would have loved as well, on a bench so that someone else could enjoy him.

"Most people would sigh at the sight of a long line," Rebecca said to Jake as he approached. "But Austin recognized it as a good thing. It means there's a bus coming soon. And as long as we're inside this rope, we're guaranteed a seat."

"Good to know," he said. "Just hope we can find the right bus. Imperial shuttle, right?"

"That's the one in the photo, yes. There are two buses, the Grand, for our hotel, and the Imperial Shuttle, which is for the sister hotel next door. They run in twenty-minute shifts. It's fifteen minutes from here to the hotel, and then they wait five minutes to load up."

"So we just need to make sure it's the Imperial?"

As soon as the words came out of his mouth, two buses pulled around the corner and looped into the pickup zone. Both buses had signs that said Adventure World, but as one slowed to a stop, the sign rotated to read Imperial Hotel.

"That's it," Rebecca said.

As the doors slowly opened, those arriving exited first. The driver climbed out and assisted a disabled passenger in loading her motorized scooter, and Rebecca realized this would give her all the time she needed to search for more clues. While most of the crowd waited in line at the front door, Rebecca and Jake peeled off toward the back of the bus and climbed on just after the passenger in the scooter.

As soon as they boarded the bus, Rebecca looked quickly at the seats and realized that row thirteen, seat W was five rows ahead. When they arrived, a pregnant woman and her two children occupied the seats in row thirteen.

"Excuse, me, I think I may have lost something," she said. "On the ride over here. Do you mind if I just check in and around the seat?"

Rebecca knew what she was looking for—or at least she thought she knew. This type of clue was something Danny had done before on the city bus that ran right by her apartment. He'd actually taken the bus the day before and planted a clue under the seat, and then Austin and Danny boarded the bus the next day and rode two stops before Austin found the clue.

The pregnant mother was empathetic to Rebecca's needs and slid over in her seat to let Rebecca check underneath. As Rebecca scooted in past the mother, she ran her hands along the seat cushion, pressing in where the backrest met the seat, and traced her fingers along the fabric until she reached the metal belt clasp. She then felt under the seat and recoiled at something cold and sticky. But Rebecca pressed on and tried again.

Jake attempted to help her by shining the light from his phone underneath the seat. Rebecca lowered to one knee, and then she saw, taped to the bottom of the seat, a long and skinny flashlight. She loosened the tape and then used the flashlight to search until she spotted a folded piece of white lined paper taped in the back corner.

She grabbed the paper and held it tight in her palm, and as she slowly rose to her feet, the pregnant woman smiled in her direction.

"Find it?"

Rebecca shook her head to indicate that she had come up short. She turned and headed to the back of the bus with Jake, and they plopped into two seats in the second-to-last row. As the doors closed, the bus became dark, and Rebecca felt the air-conditioning cool her skin. The sun was setting, but the heat was still palpable, and Rebecca relished the thought of being able to have the fifteen-minute drive back to the hotel to relax.

As she sat in the seat, she let her head fall back to the headrest and closed her eyes for one second, letting out a deep exhale. She was so exhausted she could have easily fallen asleep.

"Did you find anything?" Jake asked.

Without opening her eyes, she opened her palm and showed him the paper.

"Well done," he said. "What does it say?"

Rebecca opened her eyes, handed him the flashlight and then unfolded the clue and read. On the paper was a license plate number and the words *space 231*. Under the plate number was the name of a restaurant. Tahitian Moon.

"Wait," Rebecca said, standing up and hitting the button to signal the driver. "We need to get off this bus!"

TWELVE

Jake jumped out of his seat and hailed the bus driver as they raced to the front of the bus. He dropped the flashlight into Rebecca's backpack and helped her slip it over her shoulders just as the doors opened.

Once they had made their way to a space clear of the crowds, Rebecca handed him the clue she had found so that he could read it himself.

ILJ114
SPACE 231
TAHITIAN MOON

"These keys must unlock a car parked at the Tahitian Moon Resort. We need to get to the ferry. That's the fastest way there," Jake said.

The ferry was a mammoth white two-decker that was modeled to look like an old-fashioned steamboat. Tinted glass paneling wrapped all around the upper deck, and an American flag flew proudly on the mast. As they approached the dock, Jake noticed a crew member closing the stanchion, and he called out to him as they hustled the last few yards down the boardwalk.

"Looks like we made it just in time," Rebecca said. "Have you ever been on this ferry before?"

"Never," Jake said. "But I did hit the buffet at the Tahitian Moon one night. They've got quite the spread."

"Please do not talk about food right now," Rebecca joked. "I am absolutely starving."

"Maybe we can get something quick here once we're on the top deck? We've got at least fifteen minutes before we cross this lagoon."

Jake could tell that Rebecca was hesitant to consider doing anything that would distract her from the mission to find her son, but he knew they would need some energy, as this search was going to continue all night. As they inched forward, she noticed the No Swimming signs posted all along the edge of the lagoon, with the black silhouette of an alligator.

"Who would ever think to swim in there?" she asked.

"You never know," Jake said.

They boarded at the stern and excused themselves as they brushed by all the passengers who had taken the first seats on the lower decks and made their way toward the stairs near the bow. Up there the crowds appeared to be a little less dense, and Jake believed they would find a galley or at least some snacks to nibble on while they crossed.

They needed this moment to exhale, since they had been running nonstop the entire day. As they reached the top deck of the ferry, Jake noticed the sun setting in the sky behind them and saw how beautiful Rebecca looked in the fading light.

"This would be a great spot to watch the fireworks," he said. "And I've heard that as you cross the bay, they have lights on a lot of the boats for an on-the-water electric parade."

"Austin would absolutely love this," she said. "When I find him, I'm going to hug him and not let go for a week." She paused a moment, staring ahead, before continuing her thoughts. "I can't believe I let this happen."

Jake turned and took her by the shoulders.

"Do not, for a minute, place any of the blame of this on yourself. All you've done from the moment he disappeared has been courageous and strong. We are going to find him, and he's going to be safe because of all you have done to protect him."

Rebecca smiled as a tear welled up in her eye.

"Thanks, that means a lot. All of this means so much. I don't know where I'd be without you today."

"Of course," Jake said. "I'd do anything for you."

Rebecca leaned forward into his chest and placed her arms around his back. He held her tightly and pulled her close, where she fit so perfectly. Jake could have held her there the entire journey, but after a minute she lifted her head to ask him a question.

"So do you like living here in Florida?"

From the look in her eyes, Jake could tell she was looking for a distraction as much as any answer in particular.

"Florida's warm," he said. "But to be honest, I miss the seasons. Nothing like a true white Christmas like we had growing up."

"I agree," she said. "I wouldn't trade it for the world. So you don't see yourself settling down here?"

"No," Jake said. "Not here. Don't get me wrong, I would love to find the right person and start a family, but work has been stressful, and the truth is I just haven't found anyone I clicked with on all the right levels."

"And what is it that you're looking for?" she asked.

"Well, everything," he said. "The total package. Beauty and brains and just having fun together no matter what we're doing." In his mind he continued, *about your height, with your eyes, answers to the name Rebecca...*

As if she read his mind, she leaned in to kiss him, and Jake met her lips with his own. He held her and kissed her, and when he pulled away, her eyes were still closed.

"That was nice," she said.

"It was perfect," Jake said.

They were nearly halfway across the lagoon, and Jake noticed a few people joining a short line and walking away with hot dogs and fries. He remembered that Rebecca had mentioned how hungry she was, and although he did not want this moment to end, he knew if they were going to eat, they would have to act fast.

"Hot dogs?" he said. "Ketchup and no mustard. And a regular cola, no diet?"

He could see the smile beaming across her face.

"You remember?"

"How could I forget?" Jake said. "Working at the movie theater all those weekends, you remember your friends' favorites." He noticed a handful of others making their way to the concession line, and so he started to back away from her and head in that direction before it became too long.

"Maybe something else that we can snack on, too," she said. "Like popcorn or something light?"

Jake nodded and made his way to the snack bar. He ordered two dogs for Rebecca and two for himself, a cola for her and two waters. He also grabbed a handful of other snacks, paid, slid the tray down the counter and added the condiments, and grabbed a few napkins before turning around to head back to where they had been standing.

The entire transaction took just a minute or two, but as he turned around, he realized Rebecca was no longer standing alone where he had left her. He nearly dropped the tray to run after her before he spotted her sitting on the bench that lined the entire port side of the ferry. Seated next to her was a woman in a blue shirt, and as he moved closer, Jake recognized the woman as Charlene, the first Adventure World employee they had spoken with that morning.

As he approached them, Jake said hello and placed the tray of food down on the bench next to Rebecca, where she had been saving him a seat. She thanked him and reintroduced Charlene, and then she dropped the car keys on the tray, unzipped Austin's backpack and dropped one of the small waters inside along with the granola bars. She took a sip of the soda and then enthusiastically reached for one of the hot dogs with both hands.

"I'm so sorry," she said to Charlene. "I'm just starving."

"You need to eat," Charlene said to Rebecca before turning her attention to Jake. "We were just catching up on all you've been through."

"It's been quite a day."

"Where are you two headed now?" Charlene asked.

"We're going to check out some of the hotels across

the lagoon," Jake said, trying not to give too much of their intentions away. "We think Austin may have met up with his uncle, who is staying over this way."

"Gotcha," said Charlene as her phone buzzed and she raised it to read the incoming message. "Well, I'll keep y'all in my prayers."

She lowered her phone and began to type with her long fingernails on the screen. As she looked down, Jake refocused his attention on Rebecca.

"Once we finish eating, we should head to the stern," he said. "That way we can be first off this boat and get right over to the hotel."

Suddenly, Charlene gasped and pointed in the direction of the bow. Jake turned and instantly recognized the men in the red polo and the gray suit charging toward them.

Then, out of the corner of his eye, Jake caught Charlene swiping her hand across the tray and grabbing the keys. She leaped to her feet and took off in the direction of the two men.

"Stop," yelled Rebecca as she sprang up, tossing the food everywhere across the deck. "Stop that woman!"

The horrified passengers watched as Charlene ran between the two men and continued to the front of the boat. Just ahead Jake could see that a small motorboat had pulled up alongside the ferry, and Charlene leaned over the side and tossed the keys down to a man waiting in the boat below.

"No!" Rebecca screamed, but they did not have time to stop her. The two men were getting closer, and the one in the gray suit opened his jacket to reveal that he had found another weapon and was prepared to use it.

"Come on," Jake said, grabbing Rebecca by the hand

and running toward the back of the boat and the stairs that led to the deck below. They turned and moved through the crowd, cutting ahead of other passengers as they descended, taking two or three steps at a time. Jake quickly reversed course at the bottom of the stairs and raced Rebecca to the bow. There were fewer crowds up ahead, and so he tried to gain some distance from the two men in pursuit. Turning his head, Jake saw that red polo shirt and his partner were just coming to the bottom of the stairs, where they split up in order to surround them. Jake was running out of options.

As they reached the bow, Jake could see that on the starboard side, the ferry was within one hundred yards of one of the larger islands in the lagoon.

"I think there's only one way out of this. We swim to the island."

"What? In there? With the alligators?"

One of the men was closing in on them from the right, and red polo was making his way through the crowds from the left. Jake let go of Rebecca's hand and grabbed on the wooden railing and pulled himself up. He then reached back for her hands.

"We have to do this," he said as he lifted her onto the railing. "Pencil dive, feetfirst, and once you're in up to your waist, break the water with your hands to keep your head above water."

The man in the gray suit was only a few feet away and had his gun fully drawn. Rebecca leaped first, leaning forward but then quickly straightening her body and slicing her hands in front of her as her body splashed into the lagoon. As soon as she was in the air, Jake followed behind her, breaking the water in the same way he had instructed her. Doing this kept his head mostly above the surface and decreased the chance of injury from the height of the fall, which was just high enough that Jake believed the two men pursuing them would not attempt to follow.

Jake grabbed for Rebecca's arm and pulled her head above water.

"I'm okay," she said.

"Come on," he said as he began to swim toward the island. "Don't look back, just keep moving ahead."

Jake's years as a lifeguard made him feel secure in the fact that he could swim Rebecca to shore if he needed to do so. But she appeared to be a terrific swimmer on her own. As he had expected, the two men remained on the boat and did not attempt to dive in after them.

After the first fifty yards, Jake began to feel a cramp in his side. He lifted his head and saw that the dock on the island ahead was coming into view, and so he headed in that direction.

"We're almost there," he said.

By now the ferry, which was still continuing at full speed in the other direction, had moved far enough away that Jake no longer was worried about the two men on board. They'd last seen the motorboat on the other side of the ferry, and it appeared that it had taken off in another direction as well.

Jake imagined that surely someone had seen them go overboard and help would be on the way soon. But suddenly, as they approached the final twenty-five yards toward the dock, Jake caught a glimpse of something slithering along the shore and dipping into the water. He prayed that Rebecca had not seen it, too.

"Just keep swimming, as fast as you can," Jake said. "Head straight for that dock."

Rebecca was a strong swimmer, but in these last few yards, Jake was able to overtake her. As he approached the dock, he noticed the multiple rusty signs warning of alligators and realized that swimming was clearly prohibited, so there was no ladder to help them out of the water. This dock was designed only for boats, and so he was going to have to hoist himself out of the water.

Once he had done so, he then rolled over and extended himself back over the side of the dock and lowered his hands into the water. She was only one body length away, but Jake saw some ripples in the water just ten yards beyond her.

"Rebecca, swim right to me. With everything you've got."

Within seconds her hands were near his, and Jake grasped at her forearms to lift her out of the water. He then instructed her to put her hands around his shoulders as he swung his right hand under her back and his left arms under her legs.

"Swing your legs up onto the dock."

Rebecca propelled her torso and twisted her legs up toward the surface of the water. Her heels tapped on the wooden edge, but they did not get enough of a grip to stop her from falling back to the water.

"Again," Jake said, this time rolling himself onto his back as she kicked forward. Now there was enough momentum for her to land safely on the dock beside him.

Rebecca coughed and rolled onto her side to spit up some of the muddy water. Sitting up, she unzipped the pocket of the backpack and retrieved her water bottle and took a sip, swished it in her mouth, and then spit it out. She then handed the bottle to Jake.

"We made it," she said. "Thank God, we made it."

They hugged for a moment, but Jake realized that they were both soaking wet, and with the setting sun he knew they would not dry quickly. He took the bottom of her shirt in his hands and wrung it out.

"We need to get off this island," he said.

"What is this place?" Rebecca asked.

Jake looked to the end of the dock at the very high, locked gates adorned with barbed wire.

"Three decades ago, when it opened, this was Calypso Island. But it's been closed for years, and now it looks like they just want to make sure no one gets in."

"Or out."

Jake nodded. He wondered what remained of Calypso Island, a place that had once been home to a tropical zoo with birds and animals from around the world. As he walked to the fence and laid his fingers on the gate, he stared down the winding path and wondered if it led to the places where there were once stage shows, dining destinations and even a small, exclusive hotel. He'd heard the stories of how this place had closed abruptly fifteen years ago to remodel and then had never reopened. From what he'd heard, everything inside was preserved just as it had been, with cups still by the soda machines and mattresses still on the beds in the hotel. But Jake was convinced that was most likely the stuff of urban legend. Either way, he was glad that there was a fence between him and whatever lay on the other side.

Taking just a moment to catch their breath, Jake recapped their current situation.

"So they have the key-shaped flash drive now, along with all those other keys," Jake said. "We need to find another way back to the Tahitian Moon to see if we can catch up to them before they get too far away. The next clue must be in that car."

Rebecca smiled as she dug her hand back into the inner zippered pocket of Austin's backpack.

"I'm not sure about the next clue," she said, "but I know that the flash drive is right here." As she said the words, she removed the key-like silver drive from her pack and showed it to Jake, noting the look of surprise on his face.

"When did you do that?"

"While we were boarding the ferry," she said. "I figured that this was the real prize and that the keys to the sports car could be more of a distraction. So I took this off the key chain and I'm not letting it out of my hands until I have Austin."

"You're brilliant," Jake said.

He leaned forward and pressed his lips to hers, the exhilaration of their escape making the moment all the more intense and perfect. In that instant everything he had felt for so many years came flooding back as he touched his hand to her cheek and brushed her hair over her ear. As he pulled back, he looked into her eyes, still barely visible in the twilight, and could see that this moment meant as much to her as it had to him.

But Jake knew they had to keep moving.

Although the sun had nearly set and the lights on the island remained mostly off, some security lamps along the shore started to flicker as the darkness came. At one time this island would have been glowing like the rest of the main park, but with it abandoned, they would have to rely solely on the emergency lights and the glow of the moon to guide them.

"If we continue along here, it looks like there may be

a clearing on the other side," Jake said. "Maybe there's a way to get back to the shore from over there?"

As they climbed along the edge of the fence, Jake could make out more details of the remnants of Calypso Island. He could see the amazement on Rebecca's face as she realized just how preserved so many of the original attractions remained despite being closed for so long.

"Wow, I think I remember Austin watching some videos about this place. Some teenagers broke in and recorded and posted them online. He was obsessed."

"It's one of the great mysteries of Adventure World. So much is intact even with all the hurricanes and falling trees over so many years." As he spoke, they came to a turn and realized that the path ahead of them disappeared and the edge dropped off into the lagoon below. The path resumed ahead, but it was too great a distance for them to jump or climb, and the erosion at the end of the dock made it impossible for them to continue forward.

"So what do we do now?" Rebecca asked. "Just wait here until somebody rescues us?"

"Let's see if we can get a signal," Jake asked, tapping at his waterlogged watch, which was not responding. He reached into his pocket and retrieved both phones from his pockets, his own and the one red polo had used to call Austin. Neither would power on.

"Both dead," he said. "The water must have ruined them. Watch, too."

"Do you have a bag of rice? I heard that helps."

"Very funny," Jake said. "What about your phone?"

Rebecca reached into the backpack and retrieved her mobile that she had stored in a waterproof case.

"You think of everything," Jake said. "Where did you get that?"

"I bought this for Austin. He uses it when we're in the pool so he can keep his eye on the weather but not destroy the phone."

"Will it power on?"

"It's working," she said. "I packed a backup charger this morning. Who do we call? I'm ready to be rescued."

As Rebecca unlocked the phone to dial, Jake noticed a flicker of light just over her left shoulder. It was a small boat approaching from the west side of the island. Rebecca began to wave her hands.

"Over here!" she screamed. "Hello!"

As the boat came closer into view, Rebecca continued to call out to the approaching vessel, but Jake held out his hand to silence her.

"That's them," he said. It was the same boat that Charlene had thrown the keys into, and it was now carrying several others. Jake surmised that it was red polo and the other man, who both now appeared to have their guns drawn.

"Come on," Jake said, grabbing Rebecca by the arm and turning to race back toward the fence.

"Where are we going?" she asked. "It says No Trespassing, and it's so overgrown in there it can't be safe."

"Would you prefer the alternative?"

Jake knew that this was their only choice. He began to climb and insisted that he go first over the barbs. When he reached the top, he laid his shirt down and carefully climbed over the wires. Once he was safely on the other side, he dropped to the ground, winced a bit after landing on his sore ankle and returned his attention to Rebecca.

The boat was nearly at the dock, and the men on-board were shouting to them to freeze.

"Rebecca," he said. "Forget about them and listen to me. You need to move super slowly and be sure to just climb over this part that I'm holding down. If you do that, you'll make it through without a scratch."

He watched her as she dug her toes into the bottom rungs of the fence and began to climb. After a few steps, she became distracted by the noises of the men behind her. As she turned her head to look back, she lost her footing and slipped.

"Focus," Jake said. "Don't worry about them. Just climb."

Rebecca returned her gaze to the fence. When she reached the top, she carefully stepped over the clothing he had draped across the wires and rolled her body to the other side. She lowered herself a few rungs and then leaped to the ground. From the way she landed, Jake could tell that it hurt a bit. But she was safe on solid ground.

"I'm good," she said. "You?"

Jake nodded, though his ankle still stung from earlier in the day, and landing on it just now had not helped. But he did not have time to think as he heard the crackle of gunfire coming from the dock they had just left.

"Run!" Jake shouted. The bullets zipped past them as they ran into the darkness.

"Move like this," Jake yelled to her as he showed her how to move in a zigzag pattern to avoid their fire. Jake pointed to a path on the left that was overgrown with trees and brush. "Get up ahead of me."

Another shot rang out, and as Rebecca moved down the path, Jake stopped to draw the gun he was carrying and turned to fire back at the men. He knew it was dangerous but fortunately, the water had not damaged the gun. The lights from the dock were shining brightly now, and Jake had the cover of darkness. His bullets ricocheted off the metal fence and slowed the men down as they retreated into the bushes for cover.

At that moment, the first colors of the fireworks display exploded above them in the sky. Jake looked directly overhead to see the bursts of light seconds before he heard the eruptions of sound bursting in the night air. He realized that anyone passing by on the ferry would not hear the gunfire coming from Calypso Island as it was drowned out by Adventure World's fireworks spectacular.

Taking advantage of his position in the trees, Jake moved through the darkness to find a safe spot on higher ground. He called ahead to Rebecca.

"You keep going," he said, directing his attention to his ankle.

"I'm not going anywhere without you," she said. "We're in this together."

Rebecca had no idea where they were headed. The road beneath them felt solid, but every few steps she saw No Trespassing signs and warnings. The emergency lamps from the perimeter of the island and the glow of the moon provided only a hint of light to guide their way.

The shots Jake had fired appeared to have slowed the men who were chasing them, but Rebecca knew they would not give up their pursuit. The path they were following must have once been the main thoroughfare of the island, but as they reached the top of the hill, the road split into three directions. Rebecca took the flashlight from her bag and illuminated the top of the post to read what was inscribed upon the arrows that were pointing in multiple directions.

"Which way do we go?"

As she spoke she shone the flashlight along the buildings and grounds of this long-forgotten part of Adventure World. It was amazing. In many ways it looked the same as the Old West Ghost Town or Pirate Island— there were photo booths and drink carts and even a first aid station in the same spots where they must have been the day the island closed. But now everything was overgrown with vines, and in some places trees had fallen straight through a roof. Still, in a strange way, the buildings remained in good shape, with windows intact and walls still standing.

"What do the signs say?" Jake asked, pointing back to the pole.

Rebecca focused the beam of her flashlight on the arrows above her head.

"There's one pointing to the left," she said. "It says Birds of Prey. The one to the right says Monkey House."

"What about the other one?" he asked.

"It's pointing straight ahead. It says Hotel Calypso."

"If the hotel is in anywhere as good shape as the rest of this, I wouldn't be surprised if there were still some working utilities."

Rebecca reached for her phone. She still had some juice left, but here in the middle of the island she had no bars showing and knew that she would not have a signal to make a call. She agreed that their best option was following Jake's lead and trying to find the hotel.

As they moved down the path, they approached one of the abandoned food carts.

"It looks like it was opened one day and then closed the next," Rebecca said, scanning her flashlight beam over a soda machine. She could still clearly read the labels for each soda as if no time had passed.

Beside the cart was a sign with a map of the island. Rebecca took her phone and decided to risk taking one photo. She handed the flashlight to Jake and asked him to illuminate the map.

"If I'm reading this correctly, the hotel should be down here to the right, on the far side of the island."

"Correct," Jake whispered. "And we should probably keep our volume down as much as possible. Voices carry, and we don't want to tip them off where we are headed. And let's try to conserve that flashlight."

Rebecca agreed and shone the light ahead down the path.

"Looks pretty clear for at least a few hundred yards," she said as she turned off the beam and reached out for Jake's hand in the darkness. In many ways Rebecca was at home in the blackness. Years before her mother passed away from diabetes, she had lost her sight, and as a child Rebecca would often close her eyes to imagine seeing the world the way she did. Both Danny and Rebecca had learned to read the braille alphabet, and there were many evenings when she came home to find all the lights out, since her mother did not need them. Sometimes she left them off, reaching forward to feel for the railings and trusting herself to find her way. Tonight, as she sensed the road beneath her sloping down in a slight incline, she locked fingers with Jake, believing that he knew what lay ahead and that this man was the one who would protect her.

Behind them, in the distance, Rebecca could hear the men shouting to each other in Spanish. She imagined that they were splitting up to try and figure out where she and Jake had gone in the darkness. She snapped on the light for a few seconds when she suspected there was a tree in the path or when the road seemed to be taking a turn to the left or right, but never long enough to give them away.

At times when she shone the light, she glimpsed the abandoned cages and empty displays from the zoo. Like the rest of this island, it looked as if all the animals and birds just up and left one day. Rebecca shuddered as she considered whether some of Calypso Island's wild critters could still be here roaming around.

As they reached the edge of the island, the road became wider and was no longer hidden under the thick cover of the trees. In the bright moonlight, she could now clearly make out Jake's face and recognized what once must have been a strip of hotel rooms, about twenty or twenty-five of them, along the road. They were not enormous rooms, but Rebecca imagined that the exclusive experience of spending the night right here on Calypso Island probably made them premium rentals at one time.

Unfortunately, the hotel appeared to be in worse shape than many of the other buildings they had seen. The roof was nearly completely gone, and most of the windows had been smashed in as the result of the rough Florida hurricane seasons that had beaten down over the years. Jake motioned her to follow him up to one building with an open door.

"Let's see if there's anything electronic in there that still works," he said.

When they entered the room, Rebecca saw that there were still two queen beds in the same position they must have been in when the last guest checked out. The sheets and spreads were gone, but the beds and rotted mattresses remained. Even the television, an older, heavy tube version, still remained, though a tree branch had smashed through the glass. Across from the television, in between the beds, was a small console, and on top, as they had hoped, was a telephone.

"No way," said Jake as he approached the device. He lifted the receiver to his cheek and pressed the button to check for a dial tone. He clicked it several times, to no avail.

"Anything?" she asked.

"It's dead," he said. Behind the phone was a light switch for the room that Jake flicked on and off several times. Nothing happened.

"What now?" Rebecca asked.

Jake moved around the room to see if there was anything that could be of use to them. He opened the doors to the closet, and, amazingly, there were towels inside, neatly folded. Jake opened them up and, aside from the odor, they appeared to be perfectly fine.

He tossed one to Rebecca, and she used it to dry the remainder of her wet hair and clothes. As she looked at Jake, she saw he was ripping the towel and wrapping it around his abdomen. It was then that she noticed that he was bleeding.

"Jake," she said. "Were you shot?"

"No, I don't think so," he said while putting some pressure on the wound. "It's just a cut. From the fence."

"What are we going to do?" Rebecca asked. As she spoke, he heard the buzzing of a phone.

"Is that yours or mine?" Jake asked, taking the devices from his pocket. He looked at the still water-logged bricks and pressed his fingers on the screen. There was no response.

As the buzz sounded again, Rebecca felt it this time in her backpack. She removed her device and answered.

"Hello?"

And as she heard the voice on the other end of the line, her face began to beam with joy. "Missy, I can't believe it's you!"

THIRTEEN

Hearing Missy's voice on the other end of the line was such a comforting feeling on what had become the longest day of Rebecca's life. She pictured her brother's partner with her tight blond curls pulled back in a ponytail popping out of the back of her cap, sitting in her office in Boston wondering why Rebecca wasn't answering her phone. Maybe now Rebecca's prayers would be answered.

"Rebecca, are you still at the park? Why haven't you been picking up?"

"Missy, I'm so scared. Austin's been kidnapped."

"What?" Missy asked.

"You were right, I should have taken the protection that you offered me."

"I'm coming to get you. I hopped the first flight to Florida when we got off the phone last night. I'm at the hotel. Where are you?"

"You're here? At Adventure World?"

"Yes, at the Imperial. Where are you?" Missy asked.

"I can't even begin to tell you. I'm on an island."

"What? What island?"

Jake shot her a concerned look that warned her not

to disclose too much. But this was Missy, someone she could trust. She put her hand out and tapped Jake's arm, telling him it was okay.

"Calypso Island, I think that's the name of it. It's a part of Adventure World. Well, it was before until it closed down years ago."

"What in the world are you doing there?"

"It's a long story. We are on the run from the cartel. They took Austin, they probably have Danny and they're after us. Can you somehow get us out of here?"

"The cartel?"

"Yes. This is connected to the Velázquez cartel that Danny's been undercover with for the past year. Danny has a map or something, and now they're after us to get it back."

"You keep saying *us*. Who are you with?"

Rebecca slid her hand down to Jake's hand and squeezed.

"An old friend. Jake Foster. We've known each other since high school."

"How did you end up with him?"

Rebecca looked into Jake's eyes and smiled. "We just ran into each other. Right when I needed him the most."

"Sounds suspicious," Missy said. "Please be careful."

Rebecca laughed. "It's okay, Missy. I trust Jake as much as anyone."

"Rebecca. I told you that your brother said not to trust anyone!"

"He did."

"And he said the same thing to me. And now you have this person just mysteriously running into you on the day when your son disappears?"

Rebecca did not like where this conversation was

going. She believed and trusted Jake. After all they had been through today, there was no way he could be someone Danny was warning her about. Still, she let go of Jake's hand and took a few steps away before responding.

"I'm aware, Missy. It's fine. Now you tell me, when was the last time you spoke to my brother?"

"I texted him. About an hour ago. I haven't heard back."

"Does he usually respond right away?"

"Typically, yes. But sometimes when he's undercover like this, he can only respond when he's in the clear. Now back to you. How do I get to Calypso Island?"

"Can you get yourself to the Tahitian Moon? I believe you can rent boats from there. If you leave now, you could be here in about twenty or thirty minutes."

Rebecca moved to the back of the room, where she could see the bay through the half-demolished wall. Beyond the moon's reflection on the water, she could see the remnants of the beaches designed for the hotel guests.

"Missy," Rebecca said. "Please be careful. The cartel is after us, and they're armed. Jake and I are going to stay out of sight until you arrive."

"Have you alerted the authorities?" Missy asked.

"No, please don't. The kidnappers said they'd hurt Austin if the police were involved." Rebecca sighed. "But by this point, I'm sure park security has notified them."

Jake stepped forward to comfort her as her eyes began to fill. He mouthed the words *It will be okay.*

Rebecca wiped the back of her hand over her eyes.

"Come soon, Missy. And be safe."

"Becky, you be careful, too."

"I will," Rebecca said. "Call me when you're close. Come up on the far side of the island, away from the main dock and entrance. You'll see the beach."

"I'm not just talking about the cartel," Missy said. "Danny said we can't trust *anyone*."

Rebecca felt a knot forming in her stomach. She needed to believe in Jake but after a day like this whom could she truly trust?

"Okay," Rebecca said. "I'm going to power down my phone for twenty minutes or so, because the battery is getting low and my backup is dead, too. We may need it to find each other."

Rebecca ended the call, powered down her phone, tucked it safely into the waterproof case and returned it to Austin's backpack. It felt good that Missy was on her way, and she knew that in no time at all they would be back on the trail to find her son.

Something about that entire phone call bothered Jake at his core. Rebecca was immediately different as soon as she hung up the phone—less talkative and more distant, not looking him in the eye. Danny had warned Jake to be careful with everyone, especially his partners. Missy must have said something to Rebecca that made her lose faith in Jake, and he feared that maybe she had shared the secret he'd been withholding from Rebecca all day.

But as she caught Jake up on the details, he also thought it was incredibly strange that Danny had not mentioned anything to him about Missy, either. Had he called her before or after he made arrangements with him to be here today? Was Missy the backup plan? Was he?

"There's just something about this that doesn't add

up," Jake said. "Why would Danny ask her to arrange backup for you if he already…" Jake caught himself before he finished the sentence. But the words were already out of his mouth, and as much as he wanted to pull them back now he could not.

"If he already what?" Rebecca asked.

"It's just odd," Jake said, trying to move himself as far as possible from his slipup. "And amazing she was able to get down here so fast."

"Jake," Rebecca said. "What do you mean if he already? Already what?"

Jake breathed in slowly through his nose and exhaled quickly before he spoke. She was too smart to miss a line like that, and now the secret he had been keeping from her all day finally needed to be revealed. He lowered his head as he responded.

"Already…asked someone else."

Jake raised his head to see the look in her eyes, and even in the darkness he could tell how those words betrayed him. Rebecca's eyes filled up with tears. He reached for her hand, and instinctually she swatted it away.

"He asked *you*? You knew about this? You've known this the whole time?"

"I didn't know anything, I just—" Jake stammered before she quickly cut him off.

"You knew I was here alone with Austin? You knew someone could take him?"

"I didn't know any of that," Jake said.

"But meeting me was no accident," she said. "Like you've led me to believe all day."

"Your brother called me last night and asked me to keep an eye on you from afar."

"To spy on me?"

"No, to protect you." Jake immediately regretted his choice of words, but he could not stuff them back in his mouth.

"I don't need your protection," she said. "What I need is someone I can trust. And I thought that was you."

"It is me," Jake said.

"Yeah, right. What else have you not told me? Where is Danny?"

"Beck, I have no idea."

Rebecca turned away from him and started to walk down the rocky path toward the beach. Jake followed close behind her, as there was just enough moonlight to identify where to place one foot in front of the other. When she was several steps ahead, she continued speaking, not turning her head or looking back.

"You know, Missy was right. I need to keep away from you."

"She said that?"

Rebecca spun around, and in the half darkness Jake could see the tears running down her cheeks.

"She told me to trust no one. Just like Danny said."

"He told me that, too."

She huffed and rolled her eyes. "How do I know that? How do I know you even talked to him? You could be working for the cartel for all I know."

Jake took an extra big step and placed his hands on her shoulders. She appeared startled and recoiled at his touch.

"You need to have faith. You know that we're in this together."

"Seriously?" Rebecca said, raising the volume of her voice. This made Jake uncomfortable, knowing that

they were not completely out of danger yet, as the cartel's men were still somewhere on this island. "You're
going to talk to me about faith right now? After all the
chances you've asked me to take today? After looking
me in the eyes and leading me to believe that meeting
me here was a coincidence?"

"You're right," Jake said. "I'm sorry."

"And you're the one who never told me how you really felt about you and me. And it was you who up and
left when you came home from overseas."

Jake decided that explaining how he could not bear to
be around her if she was married to someone else was
not the right move at the moment. Anything he said was
going to come out the wrong way. As hard as it was for
him to let her words remain in the air, this silence was
probably the safest option for both of them.

They continued down the rocky path toward the
water. After a few hundred feet, the large rocks gave
way to smaller pebbles and eventually to the sand of the
beach near the lagoon. It was quiet now, and Jake could
hear the waves lapping against the rocks. In the distance
he recognized the sounds of the crowds back at Adventure World, or perhaps it was coming from the other side
near the hotels. Either way, those happy families seemed
a thousand miles away from them. Somewhere in the
distance, Missy was likely boarding her boat and on her
way to get them. And the cartel was still out there, too,
holding Austin, and maybe Danny, and waiting for Rebecca to give them what they wanted. He watched her
as she crossed over in front of him and began walking
along the sand. It had only been a few minutes since
they'd spoken, but it felt like an eternity. But Jake no-

ticed some trees near the water that would provide better cover and decided it was time to break the silence.

"We should be careful to remain up here in the trees until we see Missy and her boat," he whispered. "The cartel is still somewhere on the island, and we need to remain out of sight."

Rebecca did not respond, but she did change direction and follow him across the beach toward the wooded area. As they stepped off the path, Jake could hear the twigs crunching on the ground below. When they arrived in the shadows of the leafy palms, they crouched down so that they remained out of sight. So many thoughts raced through his head. Questions for Rebecca, information that they needed to discuss. But now was not the time.

How was he going to win back her trust? An hour ago they had shared a kiss, one that he'd been thinking about since they were in high school. And now it was all out in the open—how he had felt about her, and why he'd left. It was clear now that she'd never thought of him as more than a friend, but today had changed everything. Danny might have called to ask him to be there today, but Jake knew a force greater than that had thrust them into this adventure together. He'd believed when they kissed that this was the start of a future between them. But now all that was impossible, because he had kept the truth from her.

Never again. I will not keep anything from her again. But he knew he might have lost his chance.

Rebecca massaged her eyes and temples as she slowly breathed in through her nose and out through her mouth. Jake tried to imagine all that she must be thinking and feeling as his thoughts returned to the puzzles they had yet to solve.

First, there was Charlene, the first security guard they spoke with that morning, who then tried to steal the keys from them on the ferry. She was obviously working for the cartel, so sending them off to the Old West Ghost Town must have been a part of their plan. For some reason Jake and Rebecca needed to be distracted and kept in the park.

And then there was the cartel, who seemed to know an awful lot about Austin's and Rebecca's behaviors. Did they learn it all from hacking the Adventure World security database, finding photos of Austin, information about his profile, their quick-lane schedule and which rides they would be on at specific times? Suddenly Jake realized how all the marvelous technology could be working against them. If they'd figured this much out, what else did they already know?

Jake was relieved when Rebecca finally broke her silence.

"What will we do next, once Missy picks us up?"

Jake thought for a moment, choosing his words carefully. "We know there's another clue somewhere at the Tahitian Moon. Those keys will probably lead them to a car in a parking lot, but I have to imagine that by now they have found what they're looking for."

"I'm sure they've torn that car apart," Rebecca said. "But why would she take the keys instead of letting us find it?"

"Maybe we were taking too long?"

"And now they no longer have use for us."

Jake knew what happened to people when the cartel no longer needed them.

"No, no. Danny hid the flash drive on the key ring, and you took it off before she stole it," Jake said. "Maybe they found the car or whatever those keys will take them to, but we are the ones with the flash drive. They still need us until they recover what they want."

"For our sake, let's hope so," Rebecca said. "As soon as Missy gets here, we need to get over to that parking lot and get back on the trail." Rebecca looked at her waterproof watch. "It's nearly 10:00 p.m. We only have until midnight."

They sat for a moment in silence. In the faint light, Jake could see her attempting to make the best eye contact she could with him as she spoke in a serious tone.

"Jake, you've done enough. I don't want you to feel like you need to stay any longer than you already have."

"But, Beck, we are in this together."

The silence that lingered said more than any words could convey in that moment before Rebecca continued.

"Missy is with the DEA, and she is more than capable of looking out for me. It's been a long day, Jake. You should go home. I've got this."

"I will do whatever you need me to do," Jake said. "But maybe we keep the fact that we have the flash drive between us?"

"Between *us*?" she asked.

"I'm just not sure about Missy," Jake said. "Your brother, he told me he had suspicions about some of the people he worked with, and I think we need to as well."

"Missy is on our side."

"Let's hope so," Jake replied. "But after all we have been through today, all the deception and confusion— can we just keep that part to ourselves? Just until we're able to see what's on it."

Jake knew that this could upset her, given all that she was going through. But something just wasn't adding up for him about this entire day, and he needed more time to figure everything out.

"I'm no good with computers," she said. "I wouldn't even know what to do with this."

"In my line of work, we need to recover files like this every day," Jake said. "I could find a computer and try to see what's on it."

Rebecca reached into her pocket, and Jake could tell she was sliding her finger over the flash drive, contemplating whether she should give it to him to hold. He decided to break the ice between them and reached out his hand.

"Rebecca, if you can't trust me, then we might as well just jump back in the lagoon with the alligators."

"Alligators? Did you see alligators?"

Jake laughed. "Listen, I know you trust Missy and you are questioning me right now. But I'm not going anywhere. We are in this together, Beck. Maybe Danny asked me to help today, but I'm not here because of him."

"You're not?" Rebecca asked.

"No," Jake said. "I'm here because of you."

He met her eyes and she placed the flash drive in his hand. As he squeezed her fingers he heard the faint sound of a motor buzzing from around the north side of the island. Rebecca retrieved the phone from her pocket, and it buzzed as it powered back on.

His words, which might have meant so much an hour before, suddenly just faded into the darkness on the edge of the island as she stepped away from him and lifted the phone to her ear. Jake looked over both shoulders to make sure no one was watching them and then closed his fingers around the flash drive he was holding in his palm. He would have to work hard to fully regain her trust, but for now he savored this hint that her faith was returning. They were on a mission.

Jake walked behind her toward the boat and could barely make out Missy's directions as they approached. He knew now that no matter what happened next, things were never going to be the same.

FOURTEEN

As soon as she was in Missy's car, Rebecca started to charge her phone, and as expected, at exactly 10:00 p.m., her phone buzzed with another message from her son's captors.

Time is almost up.

In the next text, they told her to meet them in the lobby of the Adventure World Grand Hotel at midnight for an exchange—the real flash drive for her son.

Rebecca texted back a plea to let her speak with Austin. She received no reply.

The next two hours would feel like an eternity, but at least back at the hotel she could take a shower and put on some fresh clothes. Rebecca had done everything they had asked, and so far they were living up to their end of the bargain. But Rebecca had her doubts and felt as though she could not exhale until Austin was safely by her side.

It was hard for her to let go of the idea that they needed to rush to the Tahitian Moon to solve the next clue. But then she remembered that the game had changed—she had the flash drive now, so she just had to wait.

As she often did in times of great anxiety, she turned to the Lord.

Please, God, Rebecca prayed, *give me the strength to take these last steps to save my son.*

Earlier in the day, Rebecca had felt her prayers had been answered when Jake arrived. From the moment he'd appeared, she'd never felt alone. Rebecca tried to imagine anyone else on this planet whom she would have been more at home with these past twenty-four hours than Jake. She could not.

But now he had introduced doubt into the equation, and she was looking at everything from a different perspective. As great as it was that Jake had been there on the ride at the moment Austin was taken, it now appeared astonishingly suspicious. From the moment Austin was taken, there had been a series of distractions, like Charlene misdirecting them to the Old West Ghost Town when she was obviously working for the cartel. What if Jake was just another part of their plan, arriving on the scene just as Austin disappeared?

She was frustrated with her brother, too. How could he have led them into such dangerous territory? If he had even the slightest hint that Austin could be kidnapped, why wouldn't he have told Jake to stop it before it happened?

If Rebecca was beginning to explore the idea of mistrusting Jake, her friend Missy had already passed judgment. Without looking up from the road, Missy interrogated Jake, trying to trip him up with every question.

"So, Jake. How did you two meet?"

Jake laughed. "Well, it's a funny story, actually. Back in ninth grade, Danny and I were on the same hockey team, and when I came over for dinner one night after practice…"

"I meant today," Missy snapped. "How did you suddenly appear again today after so many years?"

"Jake was on the ride when it broke, when Austin was taken. He's been with me ever since."

"What a coincidence," Missy said.

"It's not entirely like that," Jake said, locking eyes with Rebecca. "Danny called me last night and told me that he didn't want Rebecca to be alone today and asked if I'd meet up with her at the park."

"Oh, so you called her and made plans to meet up?"

"Not exactly," Jake said. "He just told me where they would be and what time to meet her."

"That's odd," Missy said, turning to Rebecca. "And what did he tell you?"

"Danny knew I'd never accept help from anyone, so he asked Jake to keep an eye on me from a distance."

Rebecca sensed that Missy already knew the answer and was trying to drive a wedge between them. She understood why Missy was interrogating him, but in her heart she knew that Jake could not be working for the cartel. So before Missy had a chance to pick this apart, Rebecca changed the subject.

"So, Missy, you're staying at the Imperial?"

"It was the only place on the Adventure World property where I could stay on such short notice. Not quite as nice as where you guys are, but it's the sister hotel so I'm right next door."

When they arrived at the Adventure World Grand Hotel, it was a quarter after ten. The security gate was closed, and Missy scanned her small blue wristband in order for the arm to lift open.

"I thought you weren't staying here?" Jake said.

"The bracelets for the Imperial work on these gates, too, because it leads to both hotels," Missy said.

They walked in silence from the parking lot to the lobby and turned left toward elevators. As the doors parted, Rebecca stepped inside and leaned her back against the wall.

"I'm assuming floor fourteen?" Missy asked as she reached toward the buttons.

Rebecca smiled. Missy sure knew them well. "We got 1428. I tried for 1414, but it was booked. So I convinced him that twenty-eight was a multiple, and he was excited."

As the doors began to close, Rebecca glimpsed something in the lobby that instantly gave her a rush of adrenaline. Jake must have seen it, too, as he immediately hit the button to open the doors.

"The trains," Rebecca said as she raced toward the tracks that she recognized from the photographs.

Missy followed them to the display, completely confused. Rebecca retrieved the photograph from her backpack and attempted to explain.

"That scavenger hunt I was telling you about. We think Danny may have hidden something here in this train set."

"The map?" Missy asked. "The one on the flash drive that the cartel is after?"

"We're not sure," Jake said. "But whatever it is, it will be another clue to help us solve this mystery."

The three of them scanned the intricate replica of a real train station in a small New England town, but this was like looking for a needle in a haystack. There were thousands of tiny figurines, hundreds of buildings and mountains and tunnels that all could have held a clue. Rebecca tried to think what Austin would do if he knew there was a mystery to solve on this table. But after ten minutes, Jake suggested that they head back to the elevator.

When the doors opened on the fourteenth floor, Rebecca showed them the way to room 1428, but as soon as she lifted her wrist to scan her bracelet at the lock, she realized something was terribly wrong. The door was not fully closed, and with a gentle push of her wrist it swung open.

It was as if a cyclone had passed through the room— Austin's suitcase and personal items were strewn everywhere. Rebecca's clothes and toiletries had been emptied over one of the queen beds, and other bags containing food and dirty laundry had been tossed all over the floor.

Rebecca felt Jake's hand on her shoulder, but as she turned to him for a hug Missy quickly swept in and embraced her first. Rebecca buried her head into Missy's chest and began to weep while Missy ordered Jake to check the balcony and bathroom and make sure the room was secure.

"Rebecca, this is awful," Jake said. "But whoever was here is long gone. I can pick it up, but you should get yourself a warm shower and some new clothes so that you're at your best."

Seeing the room like this made Rebecca feel so many emotions all at once. Fear. Anger. Confusion. She felt violated.

"Maybe you could give her some space?" Missy said.

Rebecca disliked the way Missy was speaking to Jake but understood why she was so untrusting and protective. Missy was not a real fan of most men, never mind strangers who turned up in a time of crisis. It had taken her years to soften up to Danny. Rebecca nearly spoke up to suggest that it was okay for Jake to stay, but fortunately he had already read the room and took Missy up on her suggestion.

"Good idea," he said. "I'm going to head to the lobby and get myself a new shirt," he said. "Maybe I'll get a hot coffee. Anyone want anything?"

"I'm good, thanks," Rebecca said. "I think our gift shop is closed, but there's one next door, in the Imperial, that's open twenty-four hours. Take Missy's bracelet," Rebecca said, gesturing to her friend to remove her wristband. "That will get you back in the hotel if you get locked out. Knock when you get to the room, though."

Rebecca knew that Missy would not want to help Jake, but she believed this was a way to force some goodwill between them. Missy reluctantly removed the small blue band, and Jake attempted to wrap it around his wrist. When it did not fit, he stuffed it in his pocket, gave Rebecca a hug and let himself out the door.

As soon as the door had closed behind him, Missy held Rebecca squarely by the shoulders and looked her directly in the eyes.

"I don't trust him, Rebecca. We don't know anything about him."

"He's fine, Missy. We grew up together. Listen, sometimes you just know a person and can trust him. And that's how I feel about Jake."

"I'm sure there's a lot about this guy you don't know. How long has it been since you've seen him?"

"Ten, maybe eleven years? I don't know."

"I ran his name, of course. Last year he was working on an abduction. He broke protocol and the child…"

Missy caught herself before she spoke the words, but the damage was done. Rebecca imagined the very worst outcome for her son.

"Rebecca, how do you know that he's not working for these people who ransacked this room?"

"Because I trust him, Missy. I have faith in God, and I know that He sent Jake to protect me. Now, I'm going to go take a shower, and I don't want to hear another word about this when I get out. Jake Foster is a good man, and there's nothing you can say to convince me otherwise."

But even the warm water splashed on her face, Rebecca felt a chill as she recognized that she had her doubts about everything and everyone. With the water still running, she stepped out of the shower and quickly crossed the room to make sure she had locked the door.

Jake dragged his feet as he made his way down the hall to the elevator, feeling exhaustion throughout his entire body and a sadness for how he had left things with Rebecca. For the first time now he felt like a stranger in her presence. When it was just the two of them running through the park or exploring Calypso Island, it was as if no time had passed, but back here at the hotel, with Missy coming in between them, Jake felt every moment of the twelve years they had been apart.

He shook his head as he waited for the elevator doors to open, imagining the kiss they'd shared but also the look on her face when he told her the truth that he had been keeping from her. Were those sparks between them real or was it just the adrenaline pumping from their adventure together?

Jake knew Missy was probably upstairs right now tearing him apart, unraveling any remaining trust that Rebecca had in him. But there was more that bothered him about Missy than the fact she was driving a stake between them. How had Missy known exactly when to call them? The timing seemed just too perfect—too much of a coincidence. Of course, he was in no place to raise the point with Rebecca, given the fact that he had not been entirely truthful with her all day. The best thing for him to do for the moment was to keep quiet.

When he arrived at the gift shop, he poured a dark roast into a tall cup and added one sugar and two creams. He grabbed a new T-shirt off the rack and tossed it on the counter along with some gauze bandages and ointment for his wounds. It was not the worst he'd ever felt, but it was late, and freshening up a bit would certainly help him make it through the rest of the night.

He exited the gift shop through the rear entrance and turned right to head back in the direction of Rebecca's hotel when he caught a glimpse of a small business office. Despite the fact that most people brought their own laptops and every guest room had free Wi-Fi, these business spaces still remained for guests who couldn't fully escape the office and were in need of a computer or printer. As he peered inside, Jake saw a young couple printing their itineraries for the next day. He smiled and waited a moment for the couple to leave and then reached into his pocket to grasp the USB drive. He knew using a public computer was a security risk, but he had no time to waste—there could be important information on that drive that could help him solve these clues.

He sat at the desktop and followed the instructions

on the computer to log in. After looking over his shoulder to make sure he was alone, he popped the drive into the USB port on the front of the tower.

"Come on," Jake whispered in frustration as the disk whirred and struggled to load. When the folder appeared, Jake clicked to view the contents, but it was encrypted and he was prompted to enter a password. He knew too many wrong attempts could lock him out, so he ejected the drive and slipped it back into his pocket.

Jake exited the Imperial and took a detour by the outdoor pool on his way back to Rebecca's hotel. When he arrived at the main doors, he found them locked, and he scanned Missy's bracelet to unlock the gigantic doors that led into the main lobby. As he headed toward the elevators, he passed by the train table display, and in his mind he could see the image from the picture they had recovered earlier. It had been taken from this exact same viewpoint.

He approached the large table and peered through the glass to watch the moving trains below. The entire scene captured a busy New England town, complete with a bank, playground and schoolhouse. Jake thought about the video Danny had made and how he had stressed that they follow *all* the clues. Could there be something here that they had missed earlier?

As he looked at the table, he studied the miniature buildings and cars to see if anything appeared out of place. As the trains buzzed through the tunnels, Jake scanned every inch of the table, but he did not notice anything. Then, just as he was about to turn away, one of the buildings caught his eye. The art museum.

Jake remembered how in Danny's video he said that the flash drive contained maps from an art heist. He stood on to his tiptoes and leaned over the glass. With his arms fully extended, he could barely reach his fingertips to the museum building. He glanced over his shoulder to the front desk to make sure he was not being watched as he explored his hunch. He extended his fingers forward, and as he touched the miniature structure of the art museum, he felt it move in his hands. It was loose and certainly not glued to the table in the same way as all the others. It took him a few attempts, but he was able to lift it from its place. As soon as he turned the building on its side, Jake clearly saw a message taped to the bottom.

Jake removed the sliver of paper and gently returned the building to its spot in the display. He stepped away from the table and unfolded the message in his hands. He read, *"If you found the true key, then leave it here. The art belongs in the museum."*

Jake was not sure that he knew exactly what this meant, but he imagined that the key in his pocket— the flash drive—was what the clue was referring to. It didn't seem right to leave it here after all they had been through today. Rebecca had entrusted him with this USB drive, and it was the one thing that would get Austin back safely. But he thought about Danny's message to make sure they followed all the clues. Throughout this whole day, Danny's clues had led them to where they needed to be, and for some reason now he knew he needed to just believe. He popped off the roof of the museum building, and inside was a small key chain version of Worldy, the Adventure World mascot. When he removed it, there was just enough space to fit the key-shaped flash drive that was in his pocket. Jake looked over his shoulders and, feeling confident that he was alone, reached into his shorts pocket, removed the key and dropped it inside. He put the small building back together and gave it a little shake to make sure the real drive was inside before leaning forward and dropping the building back in its place in the display, the instructions to recover the priceless art securely back in the museum.

He stuffed the Worldy key chain into his pocket.

As he walked back toward the elevators, Jake felt the thrill from solving that last clue, and he trusted that God had helped him to find the place where Danny hoped he would leave the flash drive. He had no idea what the cartel would want with a Worldy key chain, but he believed that Danny had a plan and that his job now was to keep Rebecca safe and exchange it for Austin and end this nightmare.

The fourteenth floor was quiet as the elevator doors opened, and Jake whistled to himself as he walked down the hall to Rebecca's room. As he came upon the locked door, Jake could faintly hear the sound of the shower running, and as he raised his wrist to knock at the door he froze, a suspicious feeling suddenly consuming him.

Instead of knocking, Jake attempted to open the door without the wristband. Just as he figured, without the key or bracelet, the door would not budge.

He reached into his pocket and pulled out Missy's band while all at once he realized what had been bothering him since he had first seen her use it earlier. It was much too small. It belonged to a child.

As he lifted his hand to the doorknob, he heard a click and instantly the light turned green. Jake's heart raced as he knew now that his suspicions were correct.

This was Austin's band.

As the heavy door slowly opened, Jake stepped inside and reached behind his back for the weapon he was carrying. To his left he heard the shower running behind the sliding door while straight ahead he could see the nightly news playing on the television, the volume turned down low. Jake stepped forward, and as the door closed behind him, he heard the click of a gun's hammer and sensed the pistol pointing at his back.

"Don't say a word," Missy whispered from the shadows. "Just hand over your gun and walk back out that door."

FIFTEEN

Missy placed Jake's weapon in her waistband and then led him out into the hallway without lowering her own.

"You're not going to get away with this," Jake said. "Where is Austin?"

"Austin is fine," she said. "I'd never let any harm come to him. I love that boy."

"Then *where* is he?" Jake demanded. "Why do you have his wristband?"

"None of your business," Missy said as she signaled him down the hall and into the stairwell. "You've been nothing but trouble since you interfered with our plans this morning. We had this all figured out until you came along."

It suddenly began to come together for Jake. As someone Austin knew and trusted, Missy was a great asset to the kidnappers. But who else was involved?

"You keep saying *we*," Jake said. "Who are you working with?"

"Why would I tell you anything?"

"It's Lance, isn't it? He flipped to work for the cartel."

"Stop talking."

"That's what Danny figured out. That's why he couldn't trust you or anyone else back in Boston with the flash drive. His only option was to hide it in the scavenger hunt for Rebecca and Austin to find."

"You really have no idea what's actually going on," Missy said.

"So you kidnapped Austin to get back at Danny?"

"Lance did that to stop Danny from going to the authorities," Missy said. "Danny thinks the cartel has Austin, and so he's agreed to broker a deal for us with the drive."

"I thought the museum was offering a great reward," Jake said.

Missy laughed. "Try ten times what the museum is offering," she said. "As soon as we knew what we had found, there were black market offers coming from all around the globe. But Danny wanted to do the right thing and give it back to the museum. And we couldn't allow that."

"Where is Danny now?"

"He's making arrangements with the buyer," Missy said. "Lance gave him one last chance to redeem himself and save his nephew. But once he's made the introductions, he's as good as dead."

Jake knew that what lay ahead for Danny might be beyond his control, but he still did not want to believe this to be true.

"So where is the flash drive?" Missy asked as she patted down Jake's pockets. "I searched Rebecca's clothes and pack, and it's not anywhere. Charlene searched the car and couldn't find it."

Jake pictured the flash drive, hidden in the train display in the lobby thirteen floors below them.

"It's still out there," Jake said. "There are more clues

to find the drive. You need to let me go with Rebecca to solve these puzzles."

"Not on your life," Missy said. "All you've done is drag this out longer. You're useless. I did my homework on you, Jake. You blew it last year, and now you've lost again."

Her words cut through him, filling him with rage. But they also wounded him. In many ways she was right. This past year had been the hardest of his life, but these adventures today had made him feel like a hero again.

"You're wrong about me," Jake said. "And if I'm going down, then I'm taking you and Lance with me."

Suddenly, Missy's eyes darted to focus on something else as Jake heard the stairwell door open behind him. Before he could turn to react, he felt a sharp blow on the back of his head. The pain stung him instantly, and he reached with his left hand to feel the wetness at the base of his skull. Through blurry eyes he looked at his fingers, covered in blood. Jake felt weak and attempted to call for Rebecca, but when he opened his mouth, he could not say a word as he fell to the ground in a state of total darkness.

Rebecca called out to Missy as she reached for her towel. The warm shower had felt good, but she knew she only had a few minutes before they needed to meet the kidnappers for the exchange. It was troubling her how Missy spoke about Jake, but she needed them both to be on her side to get through these next few minutes until Austin's safe return.

Rebecca said a prayer to help her find her way. *Please, God, help me see the way.*

"Missy, are you there?" Rebecca asked. It was odd that she would have left the room without telling her, but maybe she went to get a drink or snack. "Jake? Are you around?"

Realizing she was alone, Rebecca dressed quickly and grabbed her backpack as well as the wristband so she could get back in the room and then headed out to look for the others.

As soon as she entered the hallway, Rebecca recognized Missy's voice coming from the stairwell. She quickly opened the door and nearly went down the stairs but froze at the top of the landing when she heard another voice coming from the floor below, a thick and gravelly Boston accent that she remembered from the earlier phone call. It belonged to Danny's old partner Lance. Rebecca crouched down, peering through the metal railing to see the figures below without being detected.

"Grab his legs there. Help me move 'im."

"Lance," Missy said, "promise you won't hurt him."

"He's an FBI agent," Lance said. "I'm not messing around."

"Whatever. Just as long as you let me take Austin back to his mother now."

Austin was here? And Missy knew where? Adrenaline surged through Rebecca's body, and it took every ounce of resistance she had not to scream and rush down the stairs to see her son. But this was all completely wrong, and Rebecca knew she had to remain in the shadows. As they moved out into the hall on the floor below, Rebecca quietly tiptoed down to the next landing to get a better view.

"The kid stays in the room, with me," Lance barked

as they moved Jake toward a guest room. "I'll send Rodriguez to meet you like we planned. When we have the drive, I'll send the kid down."

"That's not what we promised her. She's expecting to see Austin in the lobby. Without him and without Jake, she's not going to give us what we want."

"Did you search her for the drive?"

"I went through her clothes and that backpack and didn't see anything."

"You told me she would find it. You insisted that this plan would work."

"It's better than your plan, to have Charlene steal the keys."

Rebecca sneaked down a few more steps and hid so that she could still see through the glass into the hallway. Now she could more clearly see Lance, a huge bald man with muscles bulging from his black T-shirt, walking backward with his hands under Jake's armpits as Missy held his legs. Jake's body hung limp as they entered the room and shut the door behind them.

As she heard the door close, Rebecca felt safe to enter the hallway and followed them to the guest room. She pressed her ear against the cold metal. Her heart pounded as she imagined what was beyond that door. Was Jake alive? Could Austin be inside only a few feet away?

Through the door, Rebecca heard Lance continue to bark his orders.

"You need to get back upstairs. We still need her to find the drive. Charlene is useless. There was nothing in that car except another clue. You need to get Rebecca to the Tahitian Moon and start over. I'll search Foster and see what we can find."

Rebecca felt a lump in her chest as she realized they would find the flash drive with Jake, and then they would no longer have any use for him, or her, or Austin. But at this point her whole world was upside down.

It was devastating to think that Missy had deceived her, but Rebecca knew that there was a lot of money involved in recovering that stolen artwork, and that could change a person. She understood now why Danny was so skeptical of his partners and why he'd trekked all the way to Florida to bring Jake and Rebecca together to solve these clues. Jake was the only person other than Rebecca that he could trust, and she felt terrible for ever doubting him.

She knew that she had to act fast or risk losing everything she loved.

As Jake slowly regained consciousness, he realized that he was in a hotel room bathroom. But this was not Rebecca's room. His head ached, and as he reached to feel it, he realized that his right hand was handcuffed to the pipes under the sink. He slid his free hand to the top of his head and felt the dried and crusty blood in his hair.

The door to the bathroom was slightly ajar, and he could hear a television playing faintly in the distance. He heard a door open and close, and he was able to slide himself up just enough to see into the room through the opened door. He could see the time stamped in the corner of the screen on the twenty-four-hour news channel. It was 11:55 p.m. He had not been out that long, but they now only had five minutes to meet the kidnapper's demands.

But then Jake remembered what had happened just

before he lost consciousness and how all the rules had changed. Lance was alive. Missy had helped to kidnap Austin. He and Rebecca were just pawns in their game, and there was never going to be an exchange.

Just then, Jake heard the loud, screeching sounds of a fire alarm buzzing as the lights began flashing on the wall. As he slouched back down to the ground, intending to play dead, he heard Missy's voice above the noise.

"I have to get upstairs," she said. "Rebecca will hear this and come out of the shower, and I need to be there."

"I'm comin', too."

"No, she can't see you, Lance."

"Who cares?" Lance said. "It will all be over soon enough. Let's go."

Jake heard the door to the hotel room open and then close loudly behind them just as he heard the voice of a child call out above the alarms.

"What is that noise! Make it stop!"

Jake recognized Austin's voice from the phone calls earlier in the day. He was safe!

In the mirror Jake could see the reflection of a man in white walking back to the beds. Jake recognized him as the same man from the video call that morning. As he turned his head, he could see two other men as well, the man in the red polo and his accomplice in the gray suit whom Jake had last seen chasing him on Calypso Island.

"It's nothing," the man in white said to Austin. "Just go back to sleep."

"Ah," Austin said. "Make it stop!"

"Rodriguez, go find out what's going on in the hall and see if you can turn it off," the man in white said to the man in the gray suit. "And you, start getting our friend ready to move. We're going to have the fire department up here any minute, and we can't have him chained up in the bathroom."

"Where are we moving him?" Rodriguez asked.

"Doesn't matter," the man in white said. "As long as he never comes back."

"And what are we supposed to do with the kid?" the man in the red polo asked.

"He comes with us," said Rodriguez, the man in the gray suit. "His uncle has located the buyer, and we can use the kid as bait to get him to do what we want. Simple as that."

Jake heard Austin pacing back and forth in the room, repeating himself. The alarms were clearly agitating him.

"Make it stop!" Austin screamed. "Make. It. Stop!"

"Can you do something about the kid?" Jake heard the man in the red polo ask as he entered the bathroom to inspect him. "Oh, great. He's handcuffed to the sink. You got the key?"

"No," said the man in white. "Lance has it. You're going to have to improvise."

"There's a janitor's closet we just passed down the hall," Rodriguez said. "I'll find something." Jake heard the door to the room open and then close as he exited.

"We should just cut his hands off," said red polo. "If it weren't so messy."

"For the trouble he's given you, it would be worth it."

Jake smelled the stench from red polo's cigars as he came closer to inspect the situation.

"He's still out," he said. "But we don't need any tools. I think we can just unscrew the pipes and remove the trap and get him loose."

"Do something fast so then we can get out of here before the kid loses it."

As red polo reached over Jake's body to go under the sink, Jake could clearly see the gun on his hip just inches from his face. He knew he was going to have only seconds to act as soon as that pipe was loose. Red polo moved back over him and reached for a towel to enhance his grip on the P trap. Jake heard the sounds of plastic turning as red polo grunted before the coupler released and started spinning freely. Jake felt the tension ease as the water began dripping.

He reached up with his left hand and grabbed the gun from its holster while pulling his right arm free from under the sink. Red polo was shocked and surprised as Jake pulled back the hammer. The scuffle caused the man in white to come charging into the room while red polo jumped to one side. Jake hopped to his feet, whacking the man in white over the head with the butt of the gun. As he fell forward and into the bathtub, Jake turned to see the man in the red polo charging him. Jake hit him in the head as well, knocking him cold.

Then Jake heard a knock at the hotel room door. It was Rodriguez.

"What's going on in there?" he demanded.

Realizing that he had a matter of seconds before Rodriguez busted through that door, Jake looked for another way out. He quickly locked the emergency dead bolt on the door, and as he turned toward the double beds, he saw the slider to the balcony open and a small boy standing there in front of him.

"Who are you?" Austin asked. "Why do you have a gun?"

Jake looked at the weapon in his hand and realized he had to think quickly.

"It's a game," he said. "Like a video game. Do you want to play?"

The knocks at the door intensified, and the fire alarm was still chirping. Tears filled the boy's eyes as the sounds overwhelmed him.

"Open this door," Rodriguez demanded as he began to kick the door.

Jake grabbed Austin by the arm. "Come on," he said. "We need to go see your mother." As he said this, he tugged Austin in the direction of the balcony, in the same way he had guided Austin's mother so many times that day. But Austin would not budge.

"No," he said. "I'm tired. And they said I needed to stay here and be quiet if I want to see her soon."

"Austin," Jake pleaded, "I know where your mother is, and she says you need to come back to your room right away. Room 1428."

Austin's eyes lit up at the mention of the room number as Rodriguez's foot slammed into the hotel room door.

"Room 1428?" asked Austin.

"That's right," Jake said. "Fourteen twenty-eight."

Austin asked, "What room number are we in now?"

"What? I don't know."

"I just want to go check real quick," Austin said as he turned and headed toward the locked door.

"No," called Jake. "We can't go that way."

The kicks on the door were growing more forceful, and any minute that door was going to bust open.

"I want to see what number we're in," Austin demanded.

"Okay," Jake said. "But we have to go the secret way. Like in CraftWorld. We need to take a secret passage."

He'd captured Austin's attention.

"Secret passage?" Austin said. "Which way?"

"This way," Rebecca said as she entered from the balcony and scooped up the boy all in one move.

"Mommy!" Austin screamed as he leaped into her arms. Jake met her eyes with a look of surprise.

"I'll explain later," Rebecca said as she turned and carried Austin to exit the same way she had come in. "We need to move."

Once they were on the balcony, Jake followed Rebecca's directions and hopped the half wall. She handed Austin over to him before climbing the cement barrier herself. She did this quickly, keeping her son's eyes focused on the interior wall of the hotel and distracting him with a conversation. Jake looked down at the steep drop from the fourteenth floor. They had better be careful.

"Through here," Rebecca said as they landed on the balcony she had come through before. As they dashed through the room and out into the hall, Jake called out to those who were making their way to the fire exits.

"Call the police," Jake said. "Someone is chasing us."

Everyone was moving quickly to evacuate, but as soon as they set foot in the hallway and tried to move toward the stairwell, Austin's feet became cement.

"We need to go back and see what the room number is," Austin said.

"What?" said Jake.

"We need to go back," Austin insisted. "I need to see the room number again."

"We can't go back," Rebecca said. "It's too dangerous."

"Noooo," Austin said. "I need to see the room number!"

Jake attempted to pick Austin up under the arms to throw him over his shoulder, but Austin had made up his mind. He wriggled loose and ran down the hallway to see the number outside the room where he had been held captive.

Jake raced to his side while Austin studied the number on the opened door. Austin appeared to have no control over the volume of his voice or the noise he was making, and Jake pleaded with him to whisper.

"Twelve twenty-six. We were in room twelve twenty-six. There's no thirteenth floor."

"That's great," Jake said. "Now we need to go." This time, when he took Austin's hand, the boy immediately raced along with him down the hall, just as the hotel security guards and firefighters were heading in their direction and shouting at them to stop. Beyond them Jake saw Rodriguez, in his gray suit, charging in their direction.

"He's got a gun," Jake yelled, causing hotel security to turn and chase Rodriguez in the opposite direction. Jake used this diversion to whisk Austin and Rebecca into the stairwell as pandemonium erupted in the hallway. They took the stairs two at a time until they were three floors below. Jake decided to reverse course, so they exited and raced down the hallway in the opposite direction.

"Thank God, Austin," Rebecca said. "You're safe!"

"We're not safe yet," Jake said. "We need to get out of here. Now!"

When they reached the middle of the floor, Jake hit the button for the elevator. The doors would not respond.

"They won't work when there's an alarm," Rebecca said. "Let's get back to the stairs."

As they ran, Jake tried to bring Rebecca up to speed.

"Missy's working with them," Jake said. "She took Austin."

"I know," Rebecca said. "And Lance is alive, too. They're in it together. So we have Austin now. Do you still have the flash drive? Can we just go to the police?"

"No," Jake said. "But they don't have it, either."

"What do you mean?"

"There's no time to explain," Jake said. "We need to find Danny."

As he spoke her brother's name, Rebecca nearly broke into tears.

"What?"

"He's made a deal to return the drive," Jake said quietly so only Rebecca could hear. "But I think there are still more clues out there that we can follow to save him. I heard them say there were more clues in the car. We need to find them ourselves."

As soon as they reached the lobby, they raced out from the stairwell toward the back of the hotel. The front doors were swarming with police and fire and hundreds of guests in their pajamas, so Jake dashed to the back exit and onto the boardwalk that led to the other hotels. They had no choice but to find the fastest way back to the Tahitian Moon and resume solving the clues. It was their last chance to escape the danger and save their lives.

There were four other hotels within walking distance of the Adventure World Grand Hotel, and Rebecca realized that Jake was buying them some time by leading them to the one that was farthest away. They were on the run again, but now that she had Austin with her, Rebecca found a strength she had not felt all day. Still, her mind was rushing with so many questions. Where were Missy and Lance? How did Jake keep the flash drive from them? Where was Danny and how were they going to find him?

When they arrived at the Tuscan Villa Hotel, they moved quickly through to the lobby and straight to the concierge. The shuttle buses had stopped for the night, and their best option to get to the Tahitian Moon was a cab or car service. As Jake talked to the concierge, Rebecca took a moment to embrace her son.

"Are you okay, baby? Did anyone bother you today?"

"I'm great. Aunt Missy met me at the park and took me back to the hotel to play CraftWorld. Where were you?"

"Looking for you! You need to promise me that you'll never leave my side again."

"I promise," Austin said as Rebecca squeezed him tight. Before Jake walked back in their direction, she took a few moments to explain to her son who the man was who had rescued them. Jake looked so strong and handsome, and Rebecca realized in that moment that she always wanted him by her side. But how could she tell him, after all they had been through? And what if he did not feel the same way?

"Good news," he said as he joined them on the bench. "I've got us a car. It'll be here in five minutes."

"Terrific."

Jake gave her a bump of his fist. "How did you find us?"

"I hid on the stairs as Missy and Lance carried you

into that room, and I had no idea who else was inside. So I decided to draw them out."

"You pulled that fire alarm!" Jake asked.

"When everyone rushed into the hall, it created a diversion, and I snuck into one of the rooms and onto a balcony. Missy and Lance must have gone to find me upstairs while I climbed over the balconies to the room where they were holding both of you."

"That's pretty quick thinking," Jake said. "Ever consider joining the bureau?"

"Never." Rebecca smiled as the car arrived and they stood to head back out front. Jake held the door for her, and she hopped into the back seat and helped Austin with his buckle. Making sure her son was out of earshot, she leaned forward and whispered to Jake in the front seat.

"Tell me everything you know about Danny. Where is he?"

"I just overheard one of the men saying that he was arranging with a buyer and that they needed to trade for the flash drive. They were going to use Austin as bait to make Danny do what they needed."

Rebecca felt a pit in her stomach as she considered the danger that still lay ahead.

"But don't you have the flash drive? Or did Missy and Lance take it?"

"Neither. And we have your brother to thank for that," Jake said.

Rebecca was confused.

"What are you talking about?"

"Remember that photo of the train table? When I went down for coffee, I searched the table for a clue, and I found one hidden in a model of a museum. The clue was a message from Danny, and he told us to leave the flash drive there. So I did."

"You just left it there in the lobby?"

"It's hidden," Jake said. "No one will be able to find it unless they know where to look. And I did pop it into a computer, but I couldn't open it up. The files were encrypted."

"So what are we looking for now?" Rebecca asked.

"Excuse me," Austin interrupted, "what are you talking about?"

"It's just Uncle Danny's scavenger hunt," Rebecca said.

"Oh," Austin said. "Do you have more clues?"

Rebecca unzipped the backpack and retrieved the photographs and handed them to her son. He began to look through the images of the bus, the hotel lobby and the close-up of the screen.

"We need to figure these out," Jake said, turning around from the front passenger seat. "Before the other guys do."

Rebecca shot Jake a look. She didn't want him to say anything to frighten her son, but Austin was fixated on the photos. He was staring at the trains in the lobby.

"What's that photo?" Rebecca said.

"The train display from our hotel," Austin said.

"And the other one is a bus to our hotel, right?"

"Yes," Austin said. "The Grand/Imperial shuttle."

"But what about this one?" Jake said. "The blurry one. Your mom and I can't understand why this one is included."

"Always check your flash," Austin laughed. This was hilarious to him.

"What's that?" asked Rebecca.

"Always check your flash," Austin repeated. "Before you shoot."

"Is he talking about a camera?" Jake asked.

"Yes," Rebecca said as the memory suddenly rushed back to her. Danny always joked with Austin about the photos he took when the flash was overexposed and ruined the shot.

"He's trying to tell us something," Rebecca continued. "Maybe he wants us to check the flash drive."

"Like I said, it was encrypted. Could this be a clue to that password?"

"Maybe," Rebecca said. "But what could it be?"

Austin had moved on from the photos and started removing items from the backpack. He pulled out the phones, the GPS unit and the waters and granola bars. And then he blinded Rebecca when he switched on the flashlight.

Suddenly it clicked for Rebecca. She asked Austin to hand it over to Jake.

"Check this," she said. "Maybe the flashlight could be the flash he was referring to. See if there's any clues hidden inside."

Jake turned the flashlight over and unscrewed the bottom. Inside were two batteries, as expected.

"Pop those out," Rebecca said. "See if there's anything out of the ordinary."

Jake removed the batteries, but nothing looked different from any other flashlight she'd seen before. He replaced the batteries and rescrewed the base of the flashlight.

"What about the top?" she said. "Can you move anything up there?"

Jake tried the other end of the flashlight, and the bulb

turned in his hand. He slid it into his palm, and a tiny piece of paper also landed there, the size of a fortune in the cookies from the Tahitian Moon. Turning it over revealed it to be a tiny clue.

On one side it read, *Space 231*. On the other side it read, *The truth lies beneath*.

"I overheard them say that Charlene had searched the car and not found anything, just another clue," Rebecca said. "But maybe it's not in the car after all. It's under it. They were searching in the wrong place!"

"Faster," Jake said to the driver. "We need to get to the Tahitian Moon."

SIXTEEN

As their driver pulled into the parking lot, Jake found it peculiar how calm and quiet the hotel appeared as they approached the midnight hour. While there were plenty of late-night adult attractions downtown, back at the hotels, the families were mostly fast asleep in their rooms after a long day at the parks. But even though there did not appear to be anyone moving around the lot, Jake instructed the driver to pull up near the front entrance to the Tahitian Moon in case they were being watched.

Jake sneaked Rebecca and Austin along the perimeter of the hotel, snaking their way to the restaurant parking lot and the car that awaited them in parking space 231.

As soon as they were close to the numbered spot, Austin spied the convertible parked there and raced to try the door.

"Austin, no!" Rebecca cried out. But it was too late. The door opened easily, and Austin sank himself into the front driver's seat.

"This is awesome," he said.

Jake was surprised that the door was unlocked, but as he came closer he could see that Charlene and her accomplices had already paid a visit. The glove compartment was open, the rugs were ripped and overturned, and the entire back seat was pulled apart. If a flash drive or any clues were ever hidden in that car, then they had certainly been found by now. But the men in the room had said Charlene had failed, and Jake had the clue from the flashlight, something she had never seen. He walked around the outside of the car and gently laid his hand on the hood.

"The car is still in the same place," he said. "It's cold. I'd say they haven't moved it."

"So the hidden clue could still be somewhere underneath?" Rebecca asked.

"Exactly," Jake said as he fell to his knees and shone the flashlight under the car on the ground. Everything looked as it should, nothing out of place or dangerous suspended from the undercarriage. But he also saw no trace of anything hidden.

"Let's pop this in Neutral and then give it a push back," he said.

Rebecca moved to the front door of the car and ordered Austin to climb into the back seat. She shifted the car into Neutral as Jake moved to the front of the car and pushed.

After they rocked it back and forth a few times, the car began to glide backward out of the spot. Once it rolled completely out of space 231, Jake signaled to Rebecca to apply the brakes.

"That should do it," he said as he returned the beam of his flashlight to the ground in front of them. There was nothing that would have caught his attention if he had not been specifically looking for something out of the ordinary. But there, beneath the spot where one of the rear tires had been, was a loose chunk of asphalt.

"Austin," Jake said, tapping it with his toe. "See if you can move that."

The boy's fingers pried at the piece of crumbled pavement and lifted it into the air. Beneath it was a small pocket in the earth and inside the hole, Austin recovered a snack-size resealable plastic bag with a clue inside.

"What does it say?" Rebecca asked.

Austin turned himself around so that the glow of the streetlight illuminated the clue in his hand.

Rebecca, the last prize is a fake. Or perhaps it is real. The only way you will know is to see how you feel.

"The last prize?" Jake asked. "What does that mean?"

"Danny always leaves something at the end of the hunt. The grand prize. In this case, it's probably the flash drive."

"They said Charlene found a clue in the car, which we don't have. So we're at a dead end right now," Jake said. "We can't follow them without the clue."

"Unless they left it behind?"

Rebecca returned to the car and began to search frantically for any sign of a clue hidden in the car. Jake joined her, and they looked in all the usual places: the glove compartment, the center console and the trunk. They found nothing.

Jake began to pull at the upholstered fabric in the trunk before Rebecca implored him to stop.

"Danny would never have buried the clue this deep,"

she said. "He always hides them in plain sight. This is a simple game for a nine-year-old, remember."

"The game has changed." Jake said. "I think Danny knows you and I are working on this together now."

"I suppose you're right," Rebecca said. "There's no way Danny could have known all this yesterday afternoon. It's as if he's created a detour now and we are following a new set of clues."

After searching the trunk, Jake returned to look on the floor of the back seats. As he reached under the driver's side, he felt something like a ring or a hook. When he pulled out what he'd found, he dangled it in front of Rebecca to see.

"Are those the keys?" she asked, grabbing them from his hand. The ring was bent, as if someone had hastily removed something.

"Charlene and her friends must have found what they were looking for in the car and just left them behind when they were done," she said.

"I think so," Jake said. "But I think one is missing."

"Yes, there were definitely more keys before. The small shed or locker key is missing."

"So how are we going to find the locker that key went to?" Jake asked.

"Lockers?" Austin asked. "Why does everyone keep talking about lockers?"

"What do you mean, honey?" Rebecca asked.

"The men in the hotel room. They were on the phone. And they kept asking each other where there were lockers."

"Were they on speakerphone?" Jake asked. "Could you hear the conversation?"

"Yessss," Austin said, annoyed. "A woman read them a clue, and they tried to guess which lockers."

"What was the clue?" Rebecca asked. "Honey, do you remember?"

Austin shook his head no. "I was trying to play Craft-World."

"Do you remember any parts of it?" Jake asked. "Anything at all?"

"There was something about snow," Austin said. "Snow and clothes."

"A snow locker?" said Jake. "I don't get it. You store clothes in a locker. But the snow part makes no sense."

"There are lockers all over the park," Rebecca said. "But those lockers turn over every day, and they are emptied at the end of each week. Danny could not have hid anything there for the long term. And we are in Florida. Where is there snow in Adventure World?"

Jake glanced at Rebecca as she closed her eyes. He knew she was asking God for guidance. He had always admired her faith, and so he chose to join her.

Please, God, let us see the answer clearly. Where would Danny lead us? Where could he have hidden the next clue?

"Toboggan Creek!" Austin said.

Jake opened his eyes and smiled as Rebecca hugged her son. This made so much sense. Toboggan Creek was the original water park at Adventure World on land that was just beyond the Tahitian Moon Resort and Spa. Though it was once the hottest spot when it opened nearly forty years ago, the crowds began dwindling as soon as Surf City replaced it as a part of the main park expansion project. Eighteen years ago Toboggan Creek closed temporarily, and then two years later Adventure World's management announced that it was permanently closed. Now, much like Calypso Island, Toboggan Creek was overgrown and had been largely untouched by anything but nature—it was another of the great mysteries of Adventure World.

"Isn't that place condemned?" Jake asked.

"It is," Rebecca said. "It's been closed for years. But I think the lockers are just outside the fenced-off area, if I remember correctly from the videos."

"That. Is. Correct!" Austin said.

"Austin watched those videos a million times," Rebecca said. "And he memorized every aspect and detail. At first I wasn't sure they were appropriate for him, since it's all so dangerous and illegal to trespass there and film. But he was mesmerized, and once I sat down to watch the footage of the overgrown vegetation choking the old waterslides, I began to understand his obsession. There's something beautiful and mysterious about that place, untouched by visitors for decades."

"Where is it?" Jake asked.

"Ah, right over there," Austin said, pointing. "Just down that road a bit."

"Let's go," Jake said. "We'll take this car."

"All right!"

Austin was thrilled and hopped in the back seat. Rebecca climbed in beside her son, Jake started the engine and they all took off in the direction of Toboggan Creek.

As they drove Rebecca stared out the window and thought about what Jake had told her earlier, that nearly seventy-five percent of all kidnappings were by family or acquaintances of the victim. It turned out that was the case here, too. It broke her heart to feel betrayed by Missy, but at least she was in the company of a man she knew for certain she could trust.

When they were about two hundred yards away, Rebecca saw the giant gates ahead with the equally high chain-link fences topped with barbed wire and covered with No Trespassing signs. Up ahead she could see where the road bent to the left and led to what was once the best water park in all of Florida. Jake pulled the car to the side of the road and switched off the headlights. He turned the keys to silence the engine and dropped them into his pocket and laid his finger to his lips.

"We need to be extra, extra quiet," he said.

Rebecca knew that this would be no easy task with her son. Controlling the volume of his voice was not something Austin was particularly good at in most circumstances, but he was acting incredibly well-behaved tonight. Rebecca put her trust in God to guide them.

They shut the doors to the convertible gently, hardly making a sound. Jake led them into the woods, and they sneaked along the tree line until they arrived at the old locker area just outside Toboggan Creek. From there she could hear voices in the distance, but they could not make out the words. Jake suggested that Rebecca remain back with Austin while he sneaked closer, but Rebecca insisted that they stay together.

As they moved closer, Rebecca could see the figures gathered by the lockers. She recognized Missy and Lance immediately and then realized that the other woman was Charlene. She also spotted the man with the red polo and the one in the gray suit who had been chasing them all day.

Rebecca, Jake and Austin crouched down at the edge of the woods to listen. Up ahead, Lance was speaking the loudest and was directing his frustration toward Missy.

"I told you we should never have left them back at that hotel. The buyer is going to be here in less than an hour, and we have nothing to give him. I'm sick of doing things your way. All I've done is listen to you, and look where that got us."

"My way?" Missy said. "This whole thing was your idea."

"It was my idea to keep the flash drive when we recovered it as evidence," Lance said. "And to sell it to the highest bidder. But once Danny stole it from us, I wanted to kill him, and you wouldn't have it."

Rebecca's heart pulsed at the mention of Danny's name.

"Money is one thing," Missy said. "Murder is another. And you're the one who got the kid involved."

"That kid," snapped Lance. "We treated him like a king. But we should have—"

Missy cut him off before he could finish.

"Don't even think it," she said.

"That's your problem," Lance said. "You're too sentimental. You love that kid. And his mother, too."

"If that FBI agent hadn't interfered, we'd have them both now and we would have found that flash drive." Charlene spoke in an annoyed tone. "Instead we just have another one of these ridiculous clues."

"All I care about is finding that map and handing it over to the buyer," said Lance. "I don't care about clues and riddles and kids. I just want to get paid."

"Well, Danny still believes we have Austin and Jake, and he's going to bring the buyer here."

Suddenly Rebecca heard Austin's voice from behind her speaking much louder than a whisper.

"Is she talking about Uncle Danny?" Austin asked.

Rebecca spun around and tried to quiet him down. Jake grabbed her wrist to keep her low, but it was too late. As soon as Austin spoke, the beams from all the flashlights near the lockers shone directly into the woods, breaking their cover.

"Rebecca," Missy said. "Is that you?"

Jake held on to Rebecca's arm to keep her crouched with him, but she had already decided that she was done hiding. She knew they were out of options. She stood up and walked down from the trees with her hands in the air.

"Please," Rebecca said as she trudged forward and encouraged Jake and Austin to follow. "Don't hurt us."

"We won't hurt anyone. Just give us what we want," Lance said, his gun raised as he motioned them forward. "The first flash drive you found in the apple at Dino World had only half of the information we need. It's useless until we find the second one."

"We don't have another flash drive," Rebecca said.

"We need to hear that clue you found. Austin needs to hear it. That's the only way we can help you find what you're looking for."

Charlene looked to Lance, and he nodded. She raised the paper and read aloud. "'On my birthday one was born and three have died. What you are seeking is inside.'"

"Where did you find that clue?" Austin asked. "Is that from Uncle Danny?"

"Over here," Charlene said, shining her flashlight on

an opened locker compartment. "Those keys you had opened this."

"Can we see it?" Rebecca asked. Keeping herself a good distance from Lance's gun, she moved forward with her hands in the air. As she drew closer to the lockers, she thought about the clue she'd just heard and did not have any guesses. But she also thought about Danny's secret clue, the one from underneath the asphalt that was meant just for her.

Rebecca, the last prize is a fake. Or perhaps it is real. The only way you will know is to see how you feel.

Scared, she thought. *That is how I feel.*

"I have a question," Austin said, breaking the silence. "Excuse me. Where did you find that clue?"

As Rebecca approached, Charlene turned her phone's flashlight to illuminate the empty metal box.

"See," she said. "There's nothing else in there."

The metal locker was empty, but suddenly Rebecca realized that there could still be something else inside. If her twin brother was trying to send her a message that only she would be able to receive, she knew what he would do. *To see how you feel.* To read with your fingers, the way their mother felt the braille letters.

Rebecca approached the cold locker and reached her right hand inside and slid over the metal and felt the three raised bumps forming a right angle. A braille letter *F*.

"You're right," Rebecca said to the group. "There's nothing here."

As she walked back to Jake, Rebecca gave him a subtle wink.

"Enough with this," said Lance. "How do we figure out this last clue?"

"Austin," Rebecca asked. "Do you have any ideas?"

Austin bounced over to Charlene.

"Excuse me," he asked. "When is your birthday?"

"What?" Charlene asked.

"When is your birthday? I need to know to solve the clue."

Charlene looked at Missy, confused.

"Just tell him your birthday," Missy said.

"It's March twelfth," she said.

"Oh, okay," Austin said. "Three-one-two."

"But, Austin," Rebecca said. "It's not *her* birthday. She just read the clue."

"Ooh," Austin said, repeating the clue. "'On my birthday one was born and three have died. What you are seeking is inside.'"

"Inside where?" Jake asked. "Austin, do you know?"

"Of course," Austin said. "It's time to go back to Adventure World."

Lance pointed his shotgun at Jake and directed them over to his white van. Without lowering his weapon, he reached into his pocket and threw the keys to Missy.

"I'm staying here to meet Danny and the buyer," Lance said. He pointed at Rodriguez. "He's staying with me, too. The rest of you go find that drive and bring it here. Do that, and I'll consider sparing Danny's life."

Lance was a cop and Jake wanted to believe him, but he suspected Lance had crossed over long ago.

"How are we supposed to get inside Adventure World at this time of night?" Missy asked.

"Leave that to me," Charlene said.

Charlene opened the back doors of the van and ushered Jake, Rebecca and Austin inside before she slammed them shut. It was dark, cramped and crowded inside, but all Jake could think about was how Rebecca had winked at him after she put her hand in that locker. What did she know?

"Did you figure something out?" he whispered to Rebecca.

"The last prize we are going to find is a fake."

"How do you know that?"

"Inside the box I felt a letter *F* written in braille. Danny knew I would be able to read it."

"Because of your mother," Jake said.

"We learned the alphabet and a few common words."

"So if we follow these clues and find a flash drive, we will know it is a fake?"

"I guess we will figure that out when we find it," Rebecca said. "We must be getting close to the end now."

When they arrived at Adventure World's main gates, Charlene directed them down a side road that would have been barely detectable to those trying to merge into the four main lanes for the parking lot. The access road was perpendicular to the parking lot entrance and did not appear to be heading to Adventure World at all, but then it veered to the left and continued to a large parking facility underneath the main gates.

"This place runs all night," Charlene said. "Now, I'm really not supposed to be in here, but I have an ID badge from someone in the maintenance crew with that clearance. Believe it or not, there are sometimes families here at this hour on the haunted underground tour, and so we won't look all that out of place. So I'm gonna say this to y'all once. Keep your mouths shut. If anyone catches us where we're not supposed to be, it's all over."

She led them from the parking garage and through the underground tunnels. Austin looked to be beyond excited. This was his dream come true. He had memorized every passageway that had been captured and posted on the internet. He squeezed his mother's hand and bounced with a nervous energy with every step. Rebecca looked nervous, praying that he would behave. Every few yards Charlene turned and shot them a look, but overall Austin and the group remained inconspicuous.

As they came up the stairs through the double doors and into Revolution Square, Austin took the lead, and the rest of the group increased their pace to keep up.

"Does he know where he's going?" Jake asked.

"I have no doubt," Rebecca said.

"Let's think about this clue," Jake said. "'One was born and three have died.' I would think that a lot more people have been born and died than just four people, right? No matter what day it is."

"Good point," Rebecca said. "So maybe they're not people?"

"Or certain types of people? Or ideas?" Jake said. "What else can be born or die?"

Rebecca addressed Austin as he pulled ahead of them.

"Whose birthday is it? Is it someone from the park? When was the creator of Adventure World born? How would we find out?"

"April 5, 1929," Austin said.

"So is that the birthday?" Missy asked.

"No," said Austin as they approached the center of the American Heartland pavilion and the Presidential Wax Museum. "It's America's birthday."

"July Fourth," said Jake.

"And didn't Jefferson and Adams both die the same day?" Rebecca asked.

Austin bounced with excitement. "Yes, July 4, 1826."

"So who is the third who died?" Jake asked.

"The third person was James Monroe, who died on July 4, 1831."

Jake smiled at Rebecca. He was in total amazement at her son's abilities.

"So this has to be the right place," said Missy. "Great job, Austin."

It made Jake sick to think of how nice Missy was acting toward Austin, as if the past twenty-four hours had not happened and she was still "Aunt" Missy.

"So the last part of the clue is *what you are seeking is inside*," said Charlene. "Do we think the flash drive with the remainder of the map is in the Presidential Wax Museum?"

"Could be," Jake said. "Should we look somewhere around the wax figures for Adams, Jefferson and Monroe?"

Charlene led them to the door and used her stolen RFID badge to get them inside. The lights were off, and she pulled a flashlight from her pocket. Missy and Rebecca used their phones to guide them in darkness.

"We can't put the lights on," she said. "Too obvious."

As they moved slowly down the aisle, Rebecca grabbed Jake's hand. She was creeped out by the wax figures even during the day and told him that she would have avoided this attraction entirely if it were not for her son's obsession with the US presidents. As the others walked around close to the stage and examined the presidents, Rebecca led Jake to the front row, where he noticed that the seats were numbered. She was standing in front of number two.

She ran her fingers over the plush red seat.

"Two represents John Adams," she said. "The second president. Maybe something is hidden inside the seat cushion?"

Catching on, Jake searched seat three, for Thomas Jefferson.

They didn't find anything.

"Austin," Rebecca called out. "What number president was Monroe?"

"Five," Austin said.

They both ran their hands over seat five, but again there was nothing to be found.

"You think we should give up and go help Charlene and Missy?" Jake asked.

"It would have been so hard for Danny to plant anything up there on the stage," Rebecca said. "Think about how hard it would be and how different that would be from all his other clues."

"True," Jake said.

"This is ridiculous," Charlene called out from the front of the theater. "How do we even know we're in the right place?"

"We are. I know it," Rebecca said. "Can someone read the clue again?"

Missy held the clue in her hand and read, "'On my birthday one was born and three have died. What you are seeking is inside.'"

"Austin, were any presidents born on July Fourth?"

"Calvin Coolidge," Austin said. "July 4, 1872."

"That's amazing," Jake said. "I never knew that."

"But Danny did," she said. "And he knew Austin would as well."

"What number president was he?" she asked her son.

"He was the thirtieth president." Austin giggled. "Nineteen twenty-three to nineteen twenty-nine."

While everyone turned to resume their search, Rebecca moved slowly to the seat marked thirty, and Jake followed her and crouched beside her while she dug her finger into a tiny hole in the side of the seat—just large enough for a USB drive to have been shoved inside.

"Jake," she whispered. "I found it."

SEVENTEEN

"What do we do now?" Jake asked.

"I don't know. Should we tell them we found it?"

"Sometimes I trust my gut," he said. "And if the past twenty-four hours have taught me anything, it's that sometimes you need to let go and let God."

She loved that quote, and it made her feel warm inside to hear Jake speak those words. And he was right. It was time to stop trying to figure everything out and to trust that God's plan would guide them.

Rebecca nodded as she reached for Jake's hand and squeezed it tight. This man who stood beside her, who had been with her through every dangerous twist and turn, was someone she wanted to be with, always. Trust was critical to her, and Jake had been dishonest with her today, but didn't he do it to protect her and keep his promise to her brother to keep her safe? And he'd been right about Missy, and now he felt like the only person in the world she knew would never deceive her.

"Hey," she called out. "I think I've found something."

Missy and Charlene raced over as Rebecca held the drive out for them to see.

"What is it, Mommy?" Austin asked.

"I think it's a computer flash drive," Rebecca said.

"A flash drive?" Austin questioned. "That's a strange prize."

Charlene approached her quickly and swiped the drive from Rebecca's hand.

"I'll take that," she said. "You just made me a very rich woman."

"So this was all about money? Everything you've put us through, all so you could get paid?" Rebecca asked.

"I don't think you understand how much this drive is worth. Lance has a buyer who will pay us millions in cash," said Charlene.

"The operative word is *us*," Missy said as she took out her phone to text Lance the good news.

As the group retreated to the doors to the underground tunnels that would lead back to the employee garage, Rebecca began to wonder what lay ahead. What would Missy and Lance do with them now? Was there still a way to save Danny? Were they expendable now that they had served their purpose and recovered the drive? Lance could just let them go, but Rebecca feared they knew too much.

Everyone was silent for much of the ride back to Toboggan Creek. Rebecca held Austin close and leaned on Jake as they all closed their eyes. It was an incredible feeling to have this man beside her, and she tried to enjoy the moment. But she could not savor it for long as her mind drifted and she contemplated the endgame that awaited them in the abandoned water park.

Missy parked the van up against the barrier that blocked the road near the lockers at Toboggan Creek. She pulled in beside another vehicle that had not been there earlier, and Jake wondered who it belonged to. Could it be the buyer Lance had mentioned? What if it was Danny? Jake hoped and prayed that his friend was safe and that they would all be reunited soon.

As they walked toward the gates of the abandoned water park, Jake recognized a change in Missy as she communicated with Lance on the speakerphone.

"You're inside?" she said. "What are you doing in there?"

"That's what the buyer requested," Lance said. "I'm all the way at the top of the Avalanche waterslide."

"But this park is permanently closed," Austin said. "On April fourth it will be nineteen years."

"Will somebody shut that kid up?" said Charlene.

"Austin," Rebecca said, not disguising her disgust with Charlene, "we have special permission to go inside."

Following directions from Lance, Missy walked beyond the lockers and along the fence and past the large signs that read No Trespassing. The fence itself seemed to be impossible to scale, but Missy led them to a place about 150 yards into the woods, where Lance had cut a small opening in the chain links with a pair of bolt cutters that were still lying on the ground.

The only positive Jake could find in this whole idea was that they were trespassing and this action alone might draw the kind of attention they needed for a rescue. But otherwise he knew that heading into this abandoned water park spelled disaster.

"Here's what we're going to do," Missy said. "Charlene, you take these two with you inside. I'm going back to the van with Austin. The boy doesn't need to be there when this all goes down."

"Let Rebecca stay with Missy, too," Jake pleaded. "Don't separate her from her son again."

"No," Missy said. "Lance was clear. He wants both of you there for the handoff, and the boy needs to stay back with me."

Rebecca hugged Austin with a grip so tight that it took both Missy and Charlene to pull them apart.

"I will protect him," Missy said, and she directed her next words at Jake. "I know that you believe the art belongs in the museum, just like Danny wanted."

It all clicked for Jake in that moment. Missy knew he had returned the drive to the museum on the train set back at the hotel! She must have verified it out of sight from Lance, and this was her signal to him that she was on Danny's side as well.

Jake nodded and gave Austin a high five and then reached into his pocket to retrieve the small Worldy key chain he'd swapped back at the train table for the actual flash drive.

"Your uncle Danny wanted you to have this. Have fun playing with this guy until we get back," Jake said. It was as much a message to Missy as it was to Austin.

"Let's go," Charlene said, signaling to Jake and Rebecca to step through the hole in the fence.

As they crossed through to the other side, Charlene's flashlight illuminated the overgrown trees and brush, and Jake could nearly hear the echoes of thousands of children splashing and playing on the abandoned water park attractions.

"Those slides look solid," he said. "But I'm sure someone could slip right through. This place is super dangerous."

"Rumor is that people died here back in the day, and they closed down to cover that up," said Rebecca.

"Quiet!" Charlene said. "Just keep moving."

Jake stepped up onto the dilapidated wooden planks of the abandoned dock and noticed the large arrows overhead that pointed the way to the Avalanche. On his left he noticed a small, open office door; inside he could see a chair turned on its side and trash, debris and other evidence that animals had made their home there. At the end of the dock was a wooden monkey bridge secured by rope on all sides, and Charlene gestured to Jake to take the lead.

"Are we sure this is safe?" Jake asked.

"It's a better choice for you than the alternative," Charlene said, motioning with her gun.

The rope bridge felt secure to him in some spots and quite shaky in others. As they passed over the water and the rocky cliffs, Rebecca nearly lost her balance. Jake reached back to steady her before they continued on their way.

The creek they passed over was actually a pond-size man-made pool with a sandy bottom that was dyed a bit darker to add to the mystery. Now the rainwater, algae and vegetation that had overgrown the pool retained that murky bottom and made Jake fear whatever he heard splashing around in the darkness.

"Do you think Danny will be there when we arrive?" Rebecca asked.

"I'm not sure," Jake said. "But either way I'm convinced he has a plan."

At one point the path was so overgrown with trees that they could not proceed, and so they lowered themselves down a long rope and hopped back onto the ground in order to walk underneath and along the base until they reached the Avalanche Quadruple Waterslide.

"Up there," Charlene said, shining her flashlight in the direction of the long, winding staircase that led up two stories to a platform with four distinct slides descending in separate directions. "Lance said he'd meet us at the top."

Rebecca held Jake's hand as they climbed the winding stairs. The light from Charlene's flashlight allowed them the occasional glimpse into the four slides, and Jake could see they were filled with leaves, mud, overgrown branches and pools of standing water.

As they neared the top of the platform, Jake counted only two men. Lance was standing alongside the man in the red polo, who had apparently recovered from their last encounter back at the hotel.

"What is happening here?" Charlene said. "Where is the buyer?"

"Danny is bringing him here to meet me," Lance said. "Rodriguez went to watch for them."

Jake thought it was odd that they had not seen or heard them on their way in. Nothing about this felt right, and the last time he had broken protocol the child he was protecting did not survive. But this time was different. He had to trust his faith—in Rebecca, in Danny and even in Missy.

"This place does not give me a good feeling at all," Rebecca whispered. "It's a great place to make us all go missing without a trace."

"Give me the drive," Lance barked at Charlene.

"Don't do it," a voice shouted from the shadows.

"Danny!" Rebecca shouted as Charlene's flashlight

revealed that her brother was being escorted up the stairs by Rodriguez. "Are you okay?"

"He's alone," Rodriguez said. "He was sneaking around down there."

"Danny," Lance asked. "Where's your guy?"

"The buyer is back outside the gates," Danny said. "He gave me the money to exchange for the drive."

Jake thought about the real flash drive and how he had hidden it safely in the museum on the train table. Did Danny know it was back there at the hotel?

"Where did you find the drive?" Danny asked.

"In a seat cushion," Charlene said. "In the Presidential Wax Museum. These two found it for us."

"I knew that they would." Danny turned to Jake and his sister and nodded his approval. "Are you both okay? And Austin?"

"He's fine," Rebecca said. "We're fine."

"Enough talk," Lance said. "Let's do this."

"Give me the drive," Danny said.

Lance laughed. "No chance, old friend. Money first."

Danny hesitated, but when Rodriguez lifted his gun and pointed it at him, Danny reached into his pocket and pulled out a large envelope with cash that Lance quickly stepped in to retrieve. Lance signaled again for the drive. As Charlene took it from the pocket of her jeans and extended her hand to pass it to him, Rodriguez moved his aim from Danny's head and pointed the gun directly at Charlene. She placed the drive in his hand instead.

"That's it?" Rodriguez said as he looked at the tiny device in his palm. "This is what we've been after all this time?"

"It holds more information than you would imagine," Danny said. "All of the maps, photos, videos and directions. It all fits on a drive that size."

Rodriguez turned his gun toward Lance.

"I'll be keeping this," he said. "Thank you very much."

"Rodriguez," Charlene said. "What are you doing?"

"I'm the buyer," Rodriguez said. "The one Danny's been working with."

"That's impossible," Lance said. "You work for me."

Rodriguez laughed. "You fool. This whole time you thought you could steal from the FBI and then sell to the highest bidder?"

"The map was already stolen," Lance said. "By the cartel."

"And now it's going back to the cartel," Danny said. "And they keep their money. Any other solution will get us all killed."

"You snake," Lance said. "You double crosser." Lance let out a loud growl and charged at Danny. As he wrestled him to the ground, the man in the red polo turned and fired three shots in Rodriguez's direction. Rodriguez returned fire, and the man in the red polo fell to the platform. Rodriguez retrieved the envelope of cash while Jake made a move for the man in the red polo's gun. Sliding forward, he retrieved the weapon and pointed it at Rodriguez just as Lance took another swing at Danny. As Lance landed the punch, Rodriguez came in from behind him and pushed Lance back and over the side of the Avalanche's safety wall. It was only a few seconds before they heard his body hit the ground below, but Jake knew that from this height there was no way a person would survive.

Rodriguez turned and pointed the gun at Danny and motioned to Jake and the others.

"Give me your weapons, or he gets it, too," Rodriguez said.

Jake dropped the gun he had in his hand and kicked it over in Rodriguez's direction. He then looked at Charlene, who he knew was still holding her weapon.

"We can do this the easy way or the hard way. You're all of no use to me now," Rodriguez said. "Give me your weapons and I'll let you go."

"Do what he says," Rebecca pleaded. "He's got a gun to Danny's head."

Reluctantly, Charlene drew her gun from her waist and placed it on the ground. Rodriguez approached and kicked it down the slide.

"Anyone else?" Rodriguez asked.

Charlene was standing with her back against one of the slides, and as Rodriguez passed by her, she turned and flung herself down the tube. Even though it was filled with leaves and debris, it was still very slippery, and within seconds she was around a bend and out of sight. Jake could only imagine what awaited her at the bottom.

"Listen," Rebecca said, "there's no reason to kill us all."

"Oh, really," Rodriguez said. "And why is that?"

Rebecca was silent. She'd closed her eyes in this most difficult time and appeared to be praying.

Jake decided to reconnect with God as well. *Dear Lord, please guide me and give me the strength to protect this family.*

And in that moment, Jake realized what he had to do.

"Wait," Jake called out to Rodriguez. "The drive you're holding is a fake."

"Jake," Danny said. "Don't."

"If you hurt us, then you'll never find the true maps," Jake said.

"What are you talking about?" Rodriguez asked.

"He's telling the truth," Rebecca said. "It was a silver drive that was shaped like a key. I took it off the ring before Charlene stole the keys from me."

"If you let us go," Jake said, "I can take you there."

Rodriguez looked angrily at Danny.

"Why didn't you tell me any of this? Are you making a fool of me?"

"He doesn't know," Jake interjected. "He knows what he left for us to find in the scavenger hunt. But he had no idea I hid the real drive."

"Why should I believe any of this?" Rodriguez said. "You're just trying to bargain to save your lives."

"You may be right," Jake said. "But if that drive in your pocket is fake, then you're walking away from millions. If you hurt us now, you'll never be able to find the real drive."

"Okay, Mr. FBI agent. Let's go back out to my car. If you're telling me the truth, we'll find this other drive and I'll take both of them back to the cartel. But if you're lying, then that's the end for all of you."

As they retraced their steps down from the water-slides and back out of Toboggan Creek, Rebecca felt the slightest bit of hope. Austin was alive, and Rebecca prayed that Missy would never allow anyone to hurt him. Danny was here. And Jake had come up with a ruse that was keeping them all alive. At least for now.

"Move it," Rodriguez said, pointing them in the direction of the monkey bridge with his gun. When they arrived, Rebecca saw that a large rope that had once been a part of the handrail on the bridge now hung down low enough for them to use it to climb back up to the dilapidated wooden structure. Danny was the first to raise himself up, followed by Jake. It took Rodriguez a while to make the climb while keeping his gun pointed in their direction, and he had specifically left Rebecca on the ground to ensure that the other two men did not take off when they reached the top.

Rebecca looked around for a large branch or rock to throw at him as he climbed, but she feared that he would fire at them if he came under attack. When Rodriguez reached the top of the rope ladder, he instructed Rebecca to begin her ascent. She felt her hands beginning to burn as she slipped back toward the ground. The rope was swaying, and in the darkness Rebecca feared that she would hit a tree or the rope would unravel and she would drop into the ravine below.

Rebecca prayed for the strength to resume her climb. By the time she got to the top and placed her hands on the edge, she had no energy left to pull herself up. Jake raced to assist her.

"She's going to fall," he said. "Help me."

As Danny stepped forward to assist, Rodriguez fired a shot into his shoulder. Danny fell backward on the monkey bridge and braced himself against a large branch of a fallen tree. Rodriguez moved his gun back to Jake.

"Let her fall," Rodriguez said.

Rebecca felt her fingers losing their grip.

"Listen to him," she said. "Go and protect Austin. Always."

In the night she could still make out Jake's eyes, which were fixed on hers.

"Always," he said. "But you're coming with us."

Jake leaned forward and grabbed at Rebecca's fore-arms. He gave a giant tug and shouted at her to swing her legs, just as she had done hours earlier back at the dock on Calypso Island.

As she was in motion, there was a loud rustle behind Rodriguez coming from the fallen tree that was blocking the bridge. As Rodriguez turned with his gun, Charlene came charging out of the brush and tackled him. Rodriguez's gun went off as it dropped to the wooden planks, and he and Charlene wrestled to recover it.

With Rebecca safe on the side of the bridge, she hurried to her brother, who was wounded but still alive. She turned back to Jake.

"Go," he said. "Go find Austin."

"I'm not leaving you," Rebecca said.

Rodriguez's gun was on the edge of the bridge where he and Charlene were fighting, and Rebecca ran toward them and kicked it over the side. As it fell she heard it bounce off the jagged rocks below, and then she felt two hands grab her around the ankles.

Rodriguez pulled her legs out from under her, and she instantly felt the cold, hard wood of the bridge below her cheek. He then stood and pulled another gun on her, kicking her in the ribs in the direction of the edge of the bridge above the ravine. As Jake grabbed him by the shoulders, Rodriguez turned back and pointed the gun in his direction.

"Stay where you are," he said.

"Wait," Danny called out. "I have the real drive. It's in my pocket."

"What?" said Rodriguez.

"If you hurt either of them, I will toss it over the side and you'll never find it."

"I don't believe you," Rodriguez said.

Danny reached into the breast pocket of his jacket and retrieved the small key-shaped drive. He pinched it between his thumb and forefinger, and the silver device reflected in the moonlight. "This is it," he said. "This is the real prize."

"How did you get that?" Jake asked.

"You left it for me, on the train table."

As Rodriguez started to slowly approach Danny, he kept his gun pointed squarely at him. Rebecca rolled away from the edge, and Jake rushed to her side.

Apparently sensing her last chance to grab the prize in Danny's hand, Charlene leaped forward to swipe the drive from him. Rodriguez fired two shots in her direction that missed her as she slapped the drive out of Danny's hand, sending the silver metal over the edge of the bridge and into the darkness below.

As the shots sounded, the skies immediately filled with intensely bright lights. Toboggan Creek, closed for two decades, still had working emergency lights, and Jake realized that they were surrounded by a team of agents from the FBI and DEA. At the front of the group was Missy. She held her gun pointed at Rodriguez and Charlene.

"Everyone freeze," Missy ordered. Jake raised his hands, and everyone else soon followed suit.

"Officer down," Jake shouted. "And these two need to be taken away."

As Jake stood with the other agents debriefing the events of the day, Rebecca sat with Austin in the back of the fire truck, a blanket wrapped around their shoulders. She turned her head to catch a glimpse of Rodriguez, in handcuffs, as he was forced into the back of a police cruiser beside Charlene.

As Jake finished up his conversations, he headed in her direction, and when she saw him coming, Rebecca hopped down and ran to him and threw open her arms. Without hesitation they embraced, and she kissed him and felt shivers throughout her entire body as Jake passionately kissed her back. She loved this man and realized now that she always had.

"I love you, Jake."

"I love you, too."

Jake had taken a beating today, and she imagined how he must feel if his face felt as swollen and bloody as it looked.

"Looks like you'll have to put that modeling career on hold," she joked.

"Very funny," Jake said, taking a deep breath. "It's over, Rebecca. They've taken Rodriguez and Charlene into custody."

"And Lance?"

Jake nodded toward the other stretcher. "They found his body. The flash drive they were not able to locate. They're still looking."

Rebecca nodded but noticed that Jake had more to say.

"What's wrong?" she said.

"What if it's lost forever?"

"That doesn't matter," said Rebecca, putting one arm around Jake and another around her son, who had joined them. "This is all that matters."

Jake leaned in and kissed her on the forehead, and as

he pulled back, Rebecca pulled him close again. Their kiss was perfect, and she knew that there were many more in their future.

Austin seemed content playing with the toy Worldy key chain Jake had given him, and Rebecca tousled his blond curls.

"How's he holding up?" Jake asked.

"He's fine," Rebecca said. "I think he's mostly amazed that I've been inside the abandoned water park. He wants to make his own testimonial video and post it online."

"And how's Danny?" Jake asked, gesturing toward her brother.

"Let's find out," she said.

As they approached the back of the ambulance, Danny held out his hand to greet them.

"Thank you, Jake. For everything. You were the only person I could trust."

"Did you know what you were getting us into?" Jake asked.

"I began to suspect Lance was dirty when he wouldn't let us turn the drive over to the proper authorities, but I wasn't sure. So Missy and I came up with the idea to come down to Adventure World to see if he would follow us. And sure enough, he did. I knew the only thing I could do was hide the flash drive in the park until I had time to figure out a plan."

"So Missy was on your side?" Jake asked.

"The whole time. She had a careful eye on Austin, following his GPS earlier in the day and then keeping him safe once he was abducted. Missy didn't trust anyone, even you. So she stayed close to Lance so she could protect Austin, and I had you shadow Rebecca, keep her safe, follow the clues and find the map. Once you put that drive on the train table, we knew you could be trusted, too."

"But ultimately we've failed," Jake said. "The real flash drive went over the bridge and into the ravine. You think they'll ever find it?"

"No worries," Danny said. "They only cost about ten bucks at the office supply store."

Jake and Rebecca shared a look of confusion. Danny smiled and motioned for Austin to come over to join them.

"Wasn't that the drive I hid in the train table?" Jake asked. "The real one with the maps?"

"You followed the clues well," Danny said. "Both of you. Leaving that drive on the train table allowed me to bargain with him at the end. It saved our lives."

Danny motioned for Austin to share his Worldy toy key chain with him, and Austin placed it in his hand.

"But if I've learned one thing," Danny continued as he tugged at Worldy's legs to reveal that the toy was a fully functioning USB drive, "it's to always make a backup."

Jake and Rebecca looked at each other in astonishment.

"Come on," Jake said while taking Rebecca by the hand. "Let's bring this to the proper authorities so we can finally go home."

EPILOGUE

On the table in front of them was a small silver lock-box. The three-digit combination was one that Rebecca and Austin could easily crack together. And Rebecca hoped she knew what Jake had hidden inside.

It had been three months now since their adventures at the theme park. Jake had relocated to the field office just outside Boston, and they'd dined in the North End, taken a stroll through the Public Gardens and even spent a weekend on the Vineyard with Austin. They were beginning to feel like a family.

Rebecca turned her attention to the answer to the first clue. *How many towns are on Martha's Vineyard?*

"Six," said Austin, and he named them as he scrolled through the numbers. "Vineyard Haven, Oak Bluffs, Edgartown, Aquinnah, Chilmark and West Tisbury."

"Very impressive," Jake said as he smiled at Rebecca. Was there anything this kid did not know?

"Now for the second clue, how many strikes are there in a perfect game?"

"Twenty-seven," Austin said quickly and entered the number into the box.

"Six, two, seven." He tried the lock, and it would not budge.

"You're getting good at this, Jake," said Danny, who had joined them at the kitchen table.

"I learned from the best. So twenty-seven would be a perfect game in baseball, assuming that every pitch was a strike and every out was a strikeout."

"Oh, yeah," Austin said.

"And what about the other team?" asked Rebecca. "They have strikes, too."

"Good point," said Jake. "So what do you think, Austin. What other games have strikes?"

"But baseball is my favorite," he said.

"I know it is, but for this clue you should keep guessing," Jake said.

Austin thought about it for a minute before a smile took over his face.

"Bowling!"

"That's right, and what is the highest score you can get in bowling?"

"Is it three hundred?" Rebecca asked.

"Yes," Jake said. "Three hundred. So how many strikes is that?"

Austin did some quick calculations in his head.

"So with ten pins, you could have one strike in each of the first nine frames and then three more strikes in the tenth frame. That's a total of twelve strikes."

"Give it a try."

Rebecca watched with anticipation as he moved the dials—6-1-2. He slid his finger over the latch, and it clicked open. Her heart fluttered with excitement at what would be inside.

She was immediately disappointed to see a small

white envelope, which Austin opened, containing two baseball tickets.

"Baseball?" she asked. "Really?"

"It's his favorite game," Jake said.

"I'll take those," Danny said, grabbing the tickets. "What do you say, Austin? Want to go to a game tonight?"

"Yes!" He raced upstairs to find his team gear, and his uncle followed closely behind him.

Rebecca looked at Jake, cockeyed, while Jake broke into a devious smile.

"What is it?" she asked.

"You really thought I was going to make it that easy?" he said, getting down on one knee, reaching into his pocket and removing a smaller box. This one had no combination.

"There's only one question," he said. "And hopefully only one answer."

"Yes," Rebecca said, kissing him. "Yes, yes, yes. And I don't even have to look inside."

But she did. The sparkle caught her eye—her perfect man had chosen the perfect ring. Rebecca slid the beautiful round diamond onto her finger, and she hugged and kissed the man she knew she wanted to have every adventure with for the rest of her life.

* * * * *

Dear Reader,

I am so excited for you to join Rebecca and Jake on their adventure together trekking through the theme park to solve the clues and rescue her kidnapped child.

It's been a long journey for this couple, who started out as friends back in high school and who have now reunited on this mission. They must learn to trust one another as they uncover their true feelings. Their lives depend upon it.

Creating the roller coasters, rides and riddles in this story was so fun for me. I hope you enjoy your journey to Adventure World along with our characters.

Connecting with my readers is one of my greatest pleasures. Please visit me at patsyconway.com and follow Patsy Conway on Facebook or on Twitter, TikTok and Instagram using @_patsyconway.

Be well and God bless,
Patsy

Get 4 FREE REWARDS!

We'll send you 2 FREE Books plus 2 FREE Mystery Gifts.

FREE Value Over **$20**

Both the **Love Inspired®** and **Love Inspired® Suspense** series feature compelling novels filled with inspirational romance, faith, forgiveness and hope.

YES! Please send me 2 FREE novels from the Love Inspired or Love Inspired Suspense series and my 2 FREE gifts (gifts are worth about $10 retail). After receiving them, if I don't wish to receive any more books, I can return the shipping statement marked "cancel." If I don't cancel, I will receive 6 brand-new Love Inspired Larger-Print books or Love Inspired Suspense Larger-Print books every month and be billed just $6.49 each in the U.S. or $6.74 each in Canada. That is a savings of at least 16% off the cover price. It's quite a bargain! Shipping and handling is just 50¢ per book in the U.S. and $1.25 per book in Canada.* I understand that accepting the 2 free books and gifts places me under no obligation to buy anything. I can always return a shipment and cancel at any time by calling the number below. The free books and gifts are mine to keep no matter what I decide.

Choose one: ☐ **Love Inspired**
Larger-Print
(122/322 IDN GRHK)

☐ **Love Inspired Suspense**
Larger-Print
(107/307 IDN GRHK)

Name (please print)

Address   Apt. #

City   State/Province   Zip/Postal Code

Email: Please check this box ☐ if you would like to receive newsletters and promotional emails from Harlequin Enterprises ULC and its affiliates. You can unsubscribe anytime.

Mail to the Harlequin Reader Service:
IN U.S.A.: P.O. Box 1341, Buffalo, NY 14240-8531
IN CANADA: P.O. Box 603, Fort Erie, Ontario L2A 5X3

Want to try 2 free books from another series? Call 1-800-873-8635 or visit www.ReaderService.com.

---

*Terms and prices subject to change without notice. Prices do not include sales taxes, which will be charged (if applicable) based on your state or country of residence. Canadian residents will be charged applicable taxes. Offer not valid in Quebec. This offer is limited to one order per household. Books received may not be as shown. Not valid for current subscribers to the Love Inspired or Love Inspired Suspense series. All orders subject to approval. Credit or debit balances in a customer's account(s) may be offset by any other outstanding balance owed by or to the customer. Please allow 4 to 6 weeks for delivery. Offer available while quantities last.

Your Privacy—Your information is being collected by Harlequin Enterprises ULC, operating as Harlequin Reader Service. For a complete summary of the information we collect, how we use this information and to whom it is disclosed, please visit our privacy notice located at corporate.harlequin.com/privacy-notice. From time to time we may also exchange your personal information with reputable third parties. If you wish to opt out of this sharing of your personal information, please visit readerservice.com/consumerchoice or call 1-800-873-8635. **Notice to California Residents**—Under California law, you have specific rights to control and access your data. For more information on these rights and how to exercise them, visit corporate.harlequin.com/california-privacy.

LIRLIS22R3

HARLEQUIN
PLUS

Try the best multimedia subscription service for romance readers like you!

Read, Watch and Play.

Experience the easiest way to get the romance content you crave.

Start your **FREE TRIAL** at
www.harlequinplus.com/freetrial.